Lockout

(The Alpha Group Trilogy #2)

Maya Cross

Copyright © 2013 by Maya Cross
First Printing, 2013

Publisher: Maya Cross via Createspace
City: Sydney

ISBN-13: 978-1492793632

Dedicated to C.
For putting up with an awful lot.

Chapter 1

The morning after fleeing the hotel I woke, bleary eyed and exhausted, to the sound of my phone buzzing in my purse. When I'd finally found my way home it had been well after midnight and in spite of everything that had happened, I'd passed out almost instantly. A quick look at the clock told me I'd overslept.

I slipped my phone from my bag just as the ringing stopped.

12 missed calls.

I didn't even have to look at the caller ID. There was only one person who had any reason to ring that many times. I was vaguely surprised that Sebastian was so frantic. I'd figured that since the game was up, he'd admit defeat and take the opportunity to slink away quietly, but for some reason he seemed intent on fighting it out.

A night's sleep had done little to temper my anger. I hate being lied to. A tiny part of me thought that perhaps I'd overreacted, that I should have given him a chance to explain, but my past mistakes were constantly looming in my mind. I'd seen signs before and I'd turned a blind eye. I wouldn't fall into that trap again.

The phone started ringing again before I even made it to the shower. Flicking it to silent, I shoved it into my purse. I figured if I ignored him for long enough he'd eventually get the message. But I was wrong. As I was trotting out the door, I felt it vibrating against my side. And again, three minutes later, in the taxi. Twelve calls became twenty.

There was only so much I could take.

"What?" I said, answering gruffly.

"Sophia, thank god. I've been calling all morning."

"Really? I hadn't noticed."

"I didn't know what else to do. What the hell happened to you? Why did you run off?" He sounded breathless and there was a faint crack running through his voice that I'd never heard before.

"What do you care? You got what you wanted. And judging by that text message, you don't need me anymore."

"Text messa... oh Christ. Why were you looking through my phone?"

"I wasn't. I got up to get a drink and it went off behind me. Bad luck for you, hey? You nearly got away with it."

"Listen, it's not what you think—"

"Save it. Look, Sebastian, this whole thing was a mistake. I should have trusted my gut to begin with. I need you to stop calling. This is my work number and I can't have you tying up the line all day." It was a lie, but a believable one.

"Please, if you just let me come and see you for five minutes I can explain." If I didn't know better I'd have said he almost sounded desperate. It was nearly enough. Even through the phone I could feel him pulling at me like gravity. The desire to see him again was almost overpowering. But I closed my eyes and steeled myself.

"So you can sweet talk me again? No thanks. I'm done listening to your lies. Say hi to her for me."

2

"But, Sophia—"

"Goodbye."

I mashed the end call button with more vehemence than necessary. I half expected him to ring back again, but the phone remained silent.

I should have felt happy, or at least relieved, but instead I just found myself second guessing my decision. It didn't make any sense. I barely knew Sebastian. I should have been able to cut him free without breaking a sweat. But try as I might, I couldn't ignore the strange sense of loss that was forming like a grey puddle in my stomach.

As the cab pulled up to my office, I did my best to compose myself. I couldn't afford to be distracted today. After my day off, I knew my inbox would be dangerously full, and it was going to take at least an hour just to sort through.

The rest of the morning was a blur of meetings, telephone calls, and emails. Immersed in work, Sebastian gradually slipped to the back of my mind. He was still there, like a niggling splinter, but I managed to ignore him and focus on the task at hand.

It was the sort of day that seems like it will never quite end. Calls streamed in one after the other, partners who wanted information tracked down or clients needing documents drafted. My original day's work fell to the wayside as I madly attempted to juggle the new requests that were flowing in faster than I could deal with them.

It was hectic, but I have to admit there's a certain thrill to be had when you're under the gun like that. The higher the pressure, the more I enjoy my job. It's an art balancing so many tasks at once, and it's an art I excel at.

By the time the dust began to settle, it was ten o'clock. Somehow, I'd finished everything that needed doing. My stomach rumbled as I stepped out onto the street, reminding me exactly how long ago my last meal had been. There hadn't been time for such trivial things as dinner.

After wolfing down a Pad Thai from a nearby restaurant, I flopped into a cab and headed home. As the afternoon's adrenaline began to fade, I realised how wiped out I was. My fitful night's sleep and twelve hour day were catching up with me, and I still ached in several places from Sebastian's games.

Sebastian.

He hadn't called again. I didn't know if I was pleased or frustrated by that. Knowing the effect he had on me, it was probably for the best. Who knew what other lies he might have spun if given the chance. This way I could put him out of my mind and focus on what was important.

However, when the car pulled up outside my house, that plan promptly went to shit. Standing on the front porch, looking as breathtaking as ever, was the man himself.

I cursed under my breath. He couldn't have chosen a worse time. My hormones put me at enough of a disadvantage when talking to him without adding tiredness to the equation. But there was no way to avoid him now.

"Sophia," he said, as I stepped out onto the footpath. His usual look of serene confidence was gone, replaced by something darker and more drawn.

"What are you doing here, Sebastian? It's ten thirty at night."

"You said not to call, and I didn't want to upset you any more."

"So, what, you've just been waiting for me to get home?"

He nodded.

"How long have you been standing there?"

He shrugged. "I'm not sure. A few hours. It's not important. I wanted to speak to you."

It was a strangely touching gesture. But my resolve held.

"Well, I don't want to speak to you."

I took a step towards my door, but he slid in front of me, blocking my path. "Five minutes, Sophia. That's all I ask. Hear me out, and if you don't believe me, I'll leave you alone forever."

I knew from past experience how persistent he was. He wouldn't give up until I did as he wanted. I sighed. "Fine. Get on with it."

He nodded. "Thank you. Look, I'm sorry you saw what you saw, and I completely understand why you reacted the way you did. But I promise I haven't told any lies."

I raised my eyebrows and gestured for him to continue.

"That picture; it was from Hannah." I started to object, but he cut me off. "I ended things with her just like I said I had. I swear it. I had her transferred to someone else in the company, to avoid any professional conflict. I even blocked her old phone number. I did everything in my power to cut her off."

I snorted. "And so her revenge is to send you erotic photos of herself?"

He licked his lips. "She didn't take the news very well. To be honest, I've got several of those messages over the last few weeks. Judging by some of the things she's written, she thinks she can win me back, but I promise you that won't happen."

I stared at him, unsure what to think. It did make sense. I'd seen the way she looked at him. And at me, for that matter. But the best lies were always based on the truth.

"What about the girl on your wallpaper?" I asked.

He froze. For a brief moment, a look of pain crossed his face. It was gone almost as soon as it arrived, but there was no doubt I'd touched a nerve. "I didn't realise you'd seen that." He gave a small shake of his head. "She's an old flame. I'd rather not go into detail, but she's not in the picture anymore,

I promise. The photo is just something to remember her by."

So he hadn't always been the uncompromising player he was now. Someone had gotten through those walls once. Interesting.

I weighed his defence. It sounded genuine, but that was no guarantee. I'd been lied to in the past, lied to by men with sincere eyes and silver tongues. "I'm not sure if I believe you."

He began pacing. "Why would I lie? You think I'm so hard up I need to trick girls into coming to bed with me? You think I stand on porches for hours on end on the off chance it might get me laid?"

He had a point. If he was trying to deceive me, he was going to an inordinate amount of effort. "I don't know what I think anymore." I closed my eyes and shook my head. "Why me? I mean, why go to all this effort for me? You just said it yourself, you're not exactly lacking feminine attention. Hell, if what you're saying is true, Hannah would basically do anything you asked."

He exhaled heavily. "I don't know. There's something about you Sophia. I can't explain it, but the moment I saw you at our party I knew I had to have you. And after last night..." He paused, as if gathering his thoughts. "The way you taste, the way you smell, the feeling of your body underneath mine; I'm not ready to give that up."

Swallowing suddenly became difficult. In spite of all my emotional turmoil, once again he'd managed to flick that switch inside me. I swear I felt the space between us crackle to life.

"I just don't kno—" I began, but the words died on my tongue as he took two big strides towards me and seized my hands in his. With our chests just inches from each other, I was once again reminded of how big he was. His towering frame dwarfed mine, that potent magnetism washing over me

6

like a warm breeze.

"Sophia, listen to me. Last night, the things we did, the ropes, the blindfold; that takes an immense level of trust. You put yourself totally in my hands. Why can't you extend me the same trust now?"

And although I hadn't thought of it that way at the time, I realised he was right. I couldn't have done those things if I didn't trust him. Sure, I'd been afraid, but it was fear of pain, fear of the unknown, and in spite of that fear, I'd given myself to him anyway, trusting that he'd take care of me.

I realised then that I was afraid of something else too. I was afraid that Sebastian would get in his car and drive off and I'd never see him again. I didn't know why, but that fear was worse than anything I'd felt last night.

"Okay," I said quietly.

"You believe me?" The relief on his face was almost palpable.

I nodded slowly. I felt like an idiot. "I'm sorry. I should have given you a chance to explain. I don't have the best history when it comes to judging men. These days I tend to err on the side of caution... or possibly paranoia."

He looked like he wanted more details, but thankfully he didn't ask. I didn't want to have that conversation now. Later maybe, but not now. I'd already exposed him to enough of my crazy for one week. "There's nothing wrong with a little paranoia," he said instead, shooting me a smile. "It'll help keep me on my toes."

"Thanks, but I still feel stupid."

He took my hand. "Don't. I understand I'm not the easiest man to trust. I can't promise you much, Sophia, but I promise I'll never lie to you."

"That's all I can ask."

For a few seconds, I simply stood staring up into his eyes.

I still didn't really understand what had transpired between us. For someone so intent on keeping his distance, the lengths he'd gone to seemed excessive. He was a puzzle, and despite my best efforts, it looked like I'd get a little more time to solve him after all.

"You want to come in for a drink?" I asked, flashing my best provocative smile. I could feel the makings of a killer makeup sex session brewing inside me. "Maybe I can find a way to make it up to you."

He grimaced. "I wish I could, but I actually have a trip to take. Something unfortunate has happened with one of our projects, and I'm being sent down to Melbourne to sort it out."

"You can't even spare twenty minutes?" I asked, running my hand slowly down his chest.

He closed his eyes and drew a slow breath. I could almost feel the battle that was being waged inside him. "Sorry, but the plane is sitting waiting on the tarmac right now."

I rocked back in disbelief. "You held up a plane to come and talk to me?"

He shrugged. "It's our company plane, and it was only for a few hours. I didn't like the thought of leaving knowing you were upset with me."

"Well, you sure know how to make a girl feel special," I said with a laugh. "When will you be back?"

"I'm not sure. Could be a few days, could be a few weeks."

I tried my best to hide my disappointment. "Okay. Stay safe."

"I'll try." He turned and began to make his way down to the waiting car. "And Sophia, don't worry. I have a few ideas about how you can make it up to me. I'll be in touch."

There was something wicked in his smile that made the muscles between my legs clench. I had the sneaking suspicion that even from across the country, the sexy games would continue.

Chapter 2

The rest of the week passed in a familiar rhythm. It turned out that Monday's flurry of work was a sign of things to come. The phone just wouldn't stop ringing. I tried my best to get my other jobs done quickly, hoping some Wrights work would come my way, but the deluge of menial tasks simply wouldn't let up. It was frustrating. Other associates were across the hall doing something really meaningful, and I was stuck drafting settlement agreements for petty insurance claims and cleaning up my colleagues' contracts.

In spite of my busyness, Sebastian was never far from my mind. It was strange. I felt like we'd known each other a lot longer than a few weeks. It irked me to admit, but I realised that I missed him.

His text messages certainly didn't help. They started innocently enough.

Sebastian: I'm sorry I had to leave the other night. I wanted to stay, but my hands were tied.

Sophia: That's alright. I know how it is. Is everything okay down there?

Sebastian: Not really. We've had some major setbacks. Hope-fully I can get things back on track soon though. I'm already sick of being stuck down here.

I liked that he was thinking of me even when he was busy. It seemed like our argument in my office had done some good.

But as usual with Sebastian, things quickly grew hotter. I started one morning with this exchange.

Sebastian: You know, I haven't been able to get our last night together out of my head.

Sophia: Oh? =)

Sebastian: I can't wait to do that to you again. I can't wait to tie you up and fuck you until you can't even speak anymore.

Sophia: So hurry up and get back here!

Sebastian: Haha. Patience. Sometimes a little wait does a lot of good. I'm enjoying thinking of all the things I'm still yet to do to you. You have no idea how hard I'm going to make you come.

Yeah. How the hell is a girl meant to function with mes-sages like that in her inbox?

They didn't come too often, but they were just frequent enough to leave my libido on constant simmer. To make mat-ters worse, no matter how hot I got, I wasn't allowed to relieve myself. He'd made it very clear that was against the rules. Sev-eral nights when I was nearly at breaking point, I considered doing it anyway, but something stopped me. *He'd know. Somehow, he'd know.* And so I powered on and did my best to ignore it.

Because of the sheer volume of work coming in, I spent the entire weekend at the office. There were a few less people around then, and so some more meaty jobs trickled down my way, but by Monday they'd all dried up again. Finally I decided I'd had enough of sitting on the bench.

"Ernest, have you got a minute?" I said, knocking on my boss's door.

"Sophia, sure. Come in."

I shut the door behind me and took a seat in front of the desk. I never quite knew what to make of my boss. A slim, balding man of about fifty, he constantly wore a harried look, as though he were just an instant from being overwhelmed by it all. He was the law firm equivalent of middle management; reasonably competent, but totally unambitious. He'd been a partner at the firm for the last twenty years, but never seemed to care about moving any higher than that.

He'd always seemed to like me, which is why I felt comfortable going to him. His relatively lowly position meant he couldn't intervene directly to change Alan's orders, but he still held more sway than I did. If he pushed hard enough, he might be able to make something happen. Besides, I was desperate.

"I just wanted to talk to you about the Wrights case."

His eyes brightened. "It's fascinating isn't it? A real coup for us."

"I wouldn't know. I've basically done nothing but pick up the slack for the last week."

He looked a little uncomfortable. "Oh now, I'm sure that's not true."

"It is true. You know what I spent the morning doing? Cross referencing Nick and Will's notes for that fraud case."

He licked his lips. "Well, that kind of thing needs to be

done too. You know how it is, you don't always get to pick and choose what you do. Work gets given to the people best suited to the task."

"Sorry, but that's bullshit, Ernest. I'm one of the best associates on this floor and you know it. So why aren't I being allowed to help?"

His mouth curled into a sympathetic smile. "I'm not coordinating this case, Sophia. Believe me, if I were you'd be at the top of the list."

I slumped deeper into my chair. That was pretty much the response I'd been expecting. "Okay, let me ask you a different question then. Do you have any idea why Alan dislikes me so much?"

"Alan doesn't dislike you. He's just very... particular about how he does things." It was an incredibly diplomatic way of saying that he played favourites.

"Well I wish he'd be particular in my direction occasionally. Seriously, I bust my ass for this company, Ernest, and lately I get nothing in return."

He gazed at me for several seconds. "Look, how about this. I'll make some calls and see if I can't call in a few favours. But in the meantime I need you to ride this one out. If you kick up too much of a fuss you might piss off the wrong people. You know how this place is."

I felt a glimmer of hope. "That would be great, Ernest. Thanks." It probably wouldn't do much good, but it was better than nothing. "Now if you'll excuse me, I better get back to it. I think there's a child in my office who needs his school absence note drafted."

He chuckled. "Good luck with that."

Well, I'd played my hand. All I could do now was wait.

"It's something," said Ruth, when I called her a few hours later.

"Yeah. I don't think it'll amount to much though." I let out a heavy sigh. "Maybe it's just the girl factor. Maybe I need to suck it up and find a nice boutique firm somewhere where a cock isn't considered mandatory equipment for success."

"Hey, there's always a job for you here. Helping unhappy couples tear each other apart financially is rewarding in its own way."

"I'll keep that in mind," I said with a laugh, although I knew that wasn't really me. I could never do what Ruth did. It was a little too daytime chat-show for me.

"So how are things with your mystery man?" she asked. I swear I could hear her grin travelling down the phone line.

"Okay. Actually to be honest, I had a bit of a freak out, but it turned out I was just being an idiot. We talked it through, and things are good now... I think."

"You think?"

"Well, he had to fly to Melbourne for work the day we made up. We've texted a little, but I haven't actually seen him since then."

"Ah bummer. Oh well, absence makes the heart grow fonder and all that crap."

"It's not his heart I'm interested in."

She laughed. "Ah, well it can make that grow fonder too. Trust me."

I didn't sleep well that night, and the next morning I arrived at work in a foul mood. However, it didn't last long. Resting in the centre of my desk when I walked into my office was a neatly wrapped box. There was no postage stamp or delivery address. Instead, on the face, in elegant, flowing script, was a single word. *Sophia*. My heart leapt. I'd only seen that handwriting once before, in the Royal Bay, but everything about that night was etched permanently into my brain.

I walked over and picked it up, weighing it in my hands.

It wasn't particularly heavy, but there was something solid within. Shutting the door to protect from wandering eyes, I sat down at my desk and slowly peeled away the ribbon.

Rather than containing the object itself, inside the first box was another box. On top rested a note. I found myself grinning. Games within games. That was so like him.

Dear Sophia.

I'm sorry I've been gone so long. Things here are still messy and I have to stay until we can sort them out. Please forgive me.

I know I promised you a way to make up for the other day, and as much as I would like that to involve me being inside you, it will still be a few days until I return. Fortunately, I've come up with an alternative that I think you're going to enjoy.

Today I have a task for you. After you finish reading this note, I want you to sneak off into the bathroom, lock yourself in one of the cubicles, and masturbate through your panties. Play as long as you want, but our rules still stand: you're forbidden to come. Take the second box with you. When you're done, open it. There will be further instructions within. Have fun.

-S

A tingle rolled through me as I read. The request was both exciting and risky. Aside from Sebastian's kiss the other week, I'd never so much as fooled around in the office before. My job was just too important to me, and I didn't want to do anything that could come back to bite me. But the fact that Sebastian had commanded me to do it made it much more alluring. I could hear the words in his voice as I read, that strong, implacable tone that seemed impossible to resist. It was as though he was right behind me, leaning over my shoulder, strong hands lightly caressing my body as he whispered in my ear. And I felt compelled to do as I was told.

Glancing out into the corridor I saw that the building was still largely empty. Most days I tried to arrive before the bulk of my colleagues; I found that first hour of silence before the daily office buzz began was my most productive. And at that moment, it provided the perfect cover. Picking up the smaller box, I slipped casually out the door and headed for the ladies' room.

I passed a few other early-birds as I went, nodding greetings and trying to look calm. Were their smiles just friendly, or was there something smug behind them? It seemed impossible, but I couldn't shake the feeling that they knew what I was up to. It was like the fabric store all over again. I knew it was all part of Sebastian's game, but that didn't make it any easier. I clutched the box to my chest and began to walk faster, my cheeks burning with embarrassment, or excitement, or some baffling combination of the two. I'd never thought of the threat of being exposed as appealing before, but I was quickly learning that there was something strangely thrilling in that fear.

I made it to the bathroom without anyone crying foul and slipped into a cubicle with a sigh. Giving my heart a moment to settle, I sat on the toilet seat and inspected the smaller box. It was made from the same dark cardboard as the larger one, and as I tilted it from side to side, I could feel the object inside sliding around through the thin walls. Like a child on Christmas day, I began to try and guess what lay within. Judging by his request, it was probably something sexy, maybe a vibrator? Or something I might have to wear? I was incredibly curious. It took a lot of restraint not to simply tear the lid off then and there. But he'd asked me to wait, and so I did.

Instead, I reached down and hiked up my skirt, exposing my intricate pair of black lace panties. Like most girls, my underwear collection ranged from stuff I didn't wear out of the house to a few Victoria's Secret pieces I saved for special occasions. Normally for work I wore something in between, but since meeting Sebastian, my sexier pieces had been getting all the attention. As much as I hated the idea of grooming to please a guy, with his spontaneous appearances and unconventional approach, I never knew when I might need to look my best.

Masturbate through your panties. It seemed like an odd request, but I'd already learned that with Sebastian, the specifics were often important.

After listening once more to make sure there was nobody else hidden away in another cubicle, I reached out and ran a hand tentatively across my shrouded sex. Even through my underwear, I could feel how turned on I was. My juices had already begun seeping through the sheer cloth. I had no idea how he could do that to me with a simple letter, but I wasn't about to waste time considering it any further.

I began to stroke myself in a slow, steady rhythm. I was no stranger to a little fun for one. When you work the kind of hours I do, you just don't have time to seek out the real thing as often as you'd like. But this was a totally new experience. Being in a public place gave it a frenetic edge that seemed to heighten every sensation. At any moment, one of my workmates could burst in and catch me in the act. After just a minute, my heart was thundering in my chest and I could taste something sharp on my tongue.

It felt a little like I was putting on a performance. Sebastian wasn't there to see of course, but nonetheless he knew what I was doing. He knew that sometime that morning I'd be in the office bathroom, just thirty feet from my colleagues, pleasuring myself at his command. I imagined him doing the same thing, stroking that magnificent cock and picturing me. That thought drove me wild.

A moan escaped my lips as I shortened my motions, strumming my trigger with increasing urgency. The lace of the panties was rough against my skin, and the faster I rubbed the more it bit into me. Perhaps Sebastian intended it that way, perhaps he knew the kind of underwear I'd be wearing. Such precise planning wouldn't have surprised me — he'd long since proven how easily he could read me — but in truth the sensation didn't bother me. It was nothing more than a tickle compared to the delights he'd already shown me.

My breath began coming in short, sharp bursts, and a trickle of sweat lined my brow. I could feel an orgasm swelling up inside me, beckoning to me with unrestrained promise.

You're forbidden to come.

The words echoed in my head. I wanted to obey him. I knew there was a purpose behind everything he asked, a purpose that would undoubtedly lead to more pleasure later, but I was already so close. Every part of my body burned with desire. That week of waiting while my imagination ran wild seemed to have built up inside me, and now it was all bubbling to the surface. Another few seconds and I knew I'd be past the point of no return.

The tiny, logical part of my mind that wasn't flushed with hormones began to make peace with the fact that I was going to fail. He'd probably have a punishment prepared, and I doubted he'd be as gentle as last time. I might even be forced to meet the paddle. But there was nothing I could do, the pressure was too great.

Then, moments before my climax took hold, I heard the bathroom door fly open.

It was like somebody had pulled the plug out from inside

me. All the passion and arousal instantly drained away as I let out a mortified gasp. How much had they heard? I had no idea how loud I'd been. As excited as I was, it wouldn't have surprised me if the entire floor knew what I was up to. It was one thing to savour the threat of getting caught, but it was quite another for it to actually happen.

There was a pause, as though the person was deciding whether to speak.

"Are you okay in there?" she said eventually. The sing-song voice instantly sent a slinking sensation down my spine, like a wayward insect. Jennifer. I cursed silently. Of all the colleagues that I'd want to walk in on me, she was at the bottom of the list. Hell, if you threw my mother, grandmother and all my ex-boyfriends on there, Jennifer was still at the bottom.

"Hello?" she continued. "Do you need any help?"

I winced. "I'm fine. Just ate some bad prawns last night I think."

I could almost picture her face twisting into that supercilious smile as she recognised me. "Ah, Sophia, I didn't realise it was you. I hope it's not serious." Did she sound smug because she knew about my little date for one in here? Or was it just general pleasure at my discomfort? It was impossible to tell. Jennifer always sounded so damn self-satisfied.

"It's alright. I'll be fine in a couple of minutes."

"Good, good. The Wrights case is really ramping up and we need as many hands on deck as we can get. I'd hate for you to miss out because of a weak stomach." The woman's tone was saccharine sweet. I growled quietly to myself. Why wouldn't she just leave?

"I know. I wouldn't miss it for the world."

"I know you wouldn't." I heard the tap begin running, followed by the tear of paper towel. "I just came in here to freshen up. Big meeting this morning. Mister Bell himself is going to be there. Anyway, I have to run. I do hope you feel better. If you need anything, just sing out. Ta ta."

The door opened, and then the room fell silent once more. *I'd go to hell and back before I went to you for help.*

I took a deep breath and tried to calm myself. It seemed like I'd gotten away with it, although it was hard to tell with her. She'd be just as likely to keep it to herself for a few months and pull it out at an opportune moment as to rub it in my face then and there.

On the plus side, I technically hadn't disobeyed Sebastian, although it was through no strength of my own. I wondered if that counted.

Regardless, I wasn't finished yet. My eyes flicked down to where the box lay on the floor.

Take the second box with you. When you're done, open it.

I was still shaken from my near miss with Jennifer, but I scooped it up anyway. A trace of my earlier fire flared between my legs as I gazed at it. Sebastian was nothing if not inventive, and I was rapidly discovering just how much I liked his games. It was a simple gesture, classic really, an unexplained package left quietly on a desk, but he always knew how to give things just enough of a twist to set my blood pumping. Sexy commands, boxes within boxes; it was like some kind of kinky Russian doll.

Unable to wait any longer, I tugged gently at the ribbon and the box fell open. "Oh god, he didn't," I said, to no one in particular.

It had been years since I'd seen a butt plug. One past boyfriend had been more than a little fixated on my ass, so I'd consented to a little anal play. We never actually progressed to sealing the deal — it turned out my ass wasn't the only one he was fixated on — but we made it as far as a little toy play.

I didn't have the fondest memories of those times.

I exhaled sharply. In the throes of my last passionate encounter with Sebastian, I'd expressed a willingness to consider anal play, but in the cold, hard, fluorescent light of reality, the idea lost most of its charm.

I picked the plug up slowly, turning it in my hand. It wasn't particularly big — three inches long and about the thickness of a large index finger, with one end that tapered to a round point — but in the context of where it was supposed to go, it looked positively daunting.

There was another note in this box, lying next to a small white tube that I assumed was lubricant. I picked up the note gingerly.

Dear Sophia.

I trust you enjoyed that. I must admit, the thought of you pleasuring yourself kept me awake most of last night. I will definitely require a more intimate show when I return.

But the game is not quite over yet. You've obviously discovered my little gift. In my opinion, it's something every girl should own. I know you're probably a little uncertain about such things, but I think you'll come to take pleasure in them eventually. Besides, it would make me extremely happy.

I originally bought it to use on you myself, but since I've been delayed, I figured maybe you could get started without me. There's no time like the present.

With that in mind, I want you to remove your panties and place them in the box. Give the plug a healthy dose of lube and then insert it as far into your ass as you can. Don't be shy; the deeper the better. Then, I want you to return to your desk and continue working as normal.

I have no doubt it will be uncomfortable to begin with, but

21

that will pass. I love the idea of you going about your day exposed and penetrated for me. Even though I'm not there, you'll have a little piece of me inside you, a constant reminder of my presence.

You don't have to leave it in all day; it's best to start slowly. An hour or two should do it, and if you enjoy the sensation, we can go from there.

Now, if you followed my instructions properly, your panties should be in quite a state. I wish I were there to do something about that myself — I can practically taste you on my tongue right now — but seeing as I'm not, I'd like you to save them for me. You're forbidden to wear them for the rest of the day. Just keep them there in the box. And to make things a little more interesting, I'd like you to keep it on your desk until you leave. I do hope you don't get too many visitors.

I will be in touch later in the day to see that my orders have been followed. Have a lovely day.

-S

My mouth fell open as I read. The plug wasn't just a gift. He expected me to wear it right now.

My eyes darted to the lube, then back to the toy, and I swallowed loudly. Theoretically, nobody would notice — it was small, and I wasn't exactly in the habit of flashing my work mates — but still, the very idea was crazy. Walking around the office all day wearing a sex toy was about the most inappropriate thing I could think of. Except perhaps leaving a pair of sex-wet panties out on my desk. I got the sense it was more about the risk than the panties themselves, and while it was true they'd be hidden inside something, it wouldn't take much for someone to start asking questions.

But even as my rational self madly tried to dissuade me, the new Sophia, the one that had only recently awakened, was buzzing with excitement. Being commanded to do such ris-qué things was a huge turn on. It made me feel like the naughty little minx I'd never known I wanted to be. And be-yond that, it would make Sebastian happy, which was a re-ward all of its own. His pleasure became my pleasure; he'd made that very clear.

I began preparing. Breaking the seal on the lube, I squeezed a healthy dollop out onto my hand and smeared it all over the plug. *You're not basting a damn turkey,* I thought, admiring my handiwork. *That thing is going* inside your ass, *don't be stingy now.* So I took a second squeeze and did it again. Soon, I could barely keep a firm grip on the thing.

Not giving myself a chance to change my mind, I hiked up my skirt once more, slipped my underwear free, bent over, and brought the small rubber tip up to my delicate ring. The lube was cold against my skin, but the light pressure was not unpleasant. I thought back to our last night together, to the gentle probing of Sebastian's finger. In the heat of the mo-ment, I'd kind of enjoyed that. Perhaps it wouldn't be so bad.

With a deep breath I began to apply pressure. The first inch was surprisingly easy, slipping in with little resistance, but as the shaft gradually grew wider, it began to hurt. My sphincter started to spasm and tighten, rebelling against the foreign sensation. I gritted my teeth and tried to relax, but it was impossible. My body seemed to have a mind of its own. I growled in frustration.

Closing my eyes for a moment, I tried to regroup. *Think of that night in the hotel. Think of the wonderful things Sebastian still has to show you, the things he'll do to you if you please him.*

And somehow, it worked. Slowly but surely, my muscles loosened and the plug began to slide deeper. It was a lengthy process, and I stopped twice to apply more lube, but eventu-ally I buried the entire thing inside me, right down to the handle.

I let out a deep sigh, followed by a wince. The toy was as painful as I'd feared. My ass burned with the fullness of it. I experimented, shaking my hips back and forth and applying gentle pressure to the plug with my hand. Every motion sent a sting coursing through me as my muscles stretched far beyond what had been asked of them recently. It was an invasive sensation, and far from comfortable, but it was done now. Stubbornness meant I would see it through, at least for a while.

After checking that the room was empty, I slipped out of the cubicle and inspected myself in the mirror. I looked a little flustered, and somehow I'd given myself a perfect sex hair makeover despite the fact that I'd been playing solo. *Also, you're walking like you've got a stick up your ass, which I guess in a manner of speaking, you do. On the plus side, that should make you a shoe-in for partner.*

I spent a minute washing the heat from my cheeks and collecting myself, before taking another deep breath and marching out through the door. I half expected Jennifer to have gathered the entire building to witness my walk of shame, so I was pleasantly surprised to find the corridor outside empty. Perhaps I really had gotten away with it.

The walk to my desk seemed to last an eternity. Every few steps I found myself reaching out to smooth the back of my skirt, certain there was a large, plug shaped knob visible under the material. At one point, one of my colleagues decided to pop out of his office for a chat. It was one of the most excruciating conversations of my life. I could barely string two words together, and with every stumble I felt more certain I had given myself away. After a minute or so, I mumbled something about needing to go, and took off before he could stop me.

I'd never been happier to arrive at my office. Slipping inside and shutting the door, I pressed myself against it and closed my eyes. Safety.

A nervous laugh escaped my lips as I considered the lunacy of what I'd just done. Little Bell was one of the oldest and most eminent law firms in Australia. It was a company steeped in tradition, yet there I was marching the hallways with a pair of sodden panties in a box in my hands and a sex toy between my legs. It was crazy. For the hundredth time, I asked myself why I was giving Sebastian so much control, but of course I knew the answer. Because I enjoyed it as much as he did.

The next few minutes were extremely uncomfortable. Having something buried in my ass was such an alien feeling that I could barely concentrate. Several times I came close to giving up. But gradually, as my muscles began to adjust, the discomfort ebbed away. That unwavering pressure was still there, but the longer I worked, the less it bothered me.

At some point, I realised that I was actually beginning to enjoy it. It wasn't pleasurable in a direct way, but the sense of fullness was extremely satisfying. And beyond that, there was the psychological effect. Sebastian was right, the plug acted as a constant reminder of his presence. I'd be working through a dense case file, my mind utterly focused on the task at hand, when a sudden shift in position would send a wave of sensation curling through me. It was distracting, but also immensely erotic; as though he was stimulating me from across the country. The message was clear: even when we were apart, I was still his.

It was difficult to work at my normal pace. I tried my best to focus, but I couldn't slip into my normal steady rhythm. The morning's activities had left me buzzing with energy. My latent orgasm still simmered somewhere inside me, and whenever I looked up from my work, I found my eyes wandering to the box that sat just a few inches from my keyboard. It was closed of course, and looked fairly innocuous, but nonetheless it was nerve-wracking knowing that such a thing was out in the open, just waiting to be discovered. It seemed so damned obvious. I swore I could smell hints of my earlier excitement hanging in the air.

For a while it seemed like I might escape the day without any visitors, but around lunch time, I heard the dreaded sound of a knock at my door.

It was Elle. "Feel like ducking out for a bite, Soph?"

My cheeks instantly turned red. *Just chill. She probably won't even notice it.*

"I better not," I replied. "I've got a ton of stuff to do here."

She grimaced. "Bah. I guess it's me and the boys again then. I have to say, I'm getting a little tired of pretending like I give a shit about football."

"Next time," I said, smiling sympathetically.

She nodded. "Sure thing."

I thought I'd gotten away with it, but as she began to turn away, her eyes suddenly lit up. "And what have we here?" she said with a grin. "A secret admirer perhaps?"

Even though she hadn't moved, I found my hand darting out to clutch the box anyway. *Good work, Sophia. Could you be any more obvious?*

I tried to remain composed. "I wish. It's just my sister trying to make up for forgetting my birthday."

She frowned. "That was two months ago."

"What can I say? She's a crappy sister."

She studied me for several seconds, but eventually gave a short nod. "Fair enough. Get anything good?"

I breathed a silent sigh of relief. "Movie vouchers and chocolate. Original hey?"

Elle laughed. "Not really, but I wouldn't be complaining. Anyway, the others are waiting, so I better bail. I'll catch you later."

"Sure. Seeya."

Even after she'd gone, it took a few minutes for my muscles to unclench. That had been a lot closer than I'd hoped. I had to admit though, again, part of me had enjoyed the perverse thrill of coming so close to exposure. It was such a simple thing, but so naughtily creative at the same time. I had no idea where Sebastian's mind came up with such ideas.

The afternoon passed slowly. As my excitement wore off, I began to find my groove again. At about two o'clock, my desk phone rang. The caller ID showed an unfamiliar number.

"Hello," I said tentatively.

"Hello, Sophia. I hope you enjoyed your present."

I let out a little sigh. It was nice just to hear his voice again. "I did. I'm wearing it right now in fact."

"How's the fit?" he asked, his voice playful.

I laughed. "It was a little tight to begin with, but I think you got my size just right."

"Excellent. How about my other requests?"

"All done."

"I'm impressed. Had any close calls?"

"One, but I dealt with it."

He chuckled. "I'm glad to hear it."

I hesitated, choosing my words carefully, not wanting to sound too needy. "So how's the trip? Are you nearly done there?"

"A few more days probably. There's still one or two things to take care of."

"Good, because after this morning, I'm thoroughly in need of a good seeing to."

He laughed. "I know the feeling. Christ, I'm hard just thinking about you sitting there with no panties on. But in any case, good behaviour deserves a reward. Since you did such a wonderful job this morning, I'm going to lift the rules. You're free to come as many times as you want until I return."

I blew out a slow breath. Part of me wanted to run back to the bathroom that very moment and finish what I'd started. But I restrained myself. "Are you sure?"

"Yes. You've earned it. But save a little something for me. I've got plans for you when I get back."

"I'll do my best. And you should know, I'll be thinking of you the whole time."

"I would expect nothing else," he said. "On another note, I saw on the news yesterday that your firm has picked up that big pharmaceutical class action suit. I bet that's pretty exciting."

I sighed. What a way to kill the mood. "It is, for the people working on it."

"And I take it by your tone that you're not one of them?"

"Not at the moment."

"I'm sorry, Sophia."

"Hey, it's okay, I'm used to it," I replied. "Anyway, I should go. I may not be working on Wrights, but I have a pile of other stuff to do."

"No problem. I'll be in touch when I get back. Have a good night."

"I most certainly will. Bye."

Knowing I had Sebastian's blessing to relieve the pressure made the rest of the day a little easier. I got through everything I had to do by six o'clock.

I think I was beginning to appreciate the new side of me

that Sebastian was gradually teasing out, because I found the walk out with no underwear on immensely enjoyable. It was my little secret that nobody else knew, and it made even the simple act of saying goodbye to people sexy. Plus I knew that somewhere, a thousand kilometres away, it was driving Sebastian crazy, which made it hotter still.

A few people tried to stop me on my way out to chat, but I politely excused myself. I had more important things on my agenda. Like a long overdue date with a battery operated friend.

Chapter 3

The next night, I gave myself an early mark and headed home from the office at five on the dot. If they weren't going to assign me the work I wanted, I sure as hell wasn't giving them maximum effort. I decided a little me-time was in order.

After taking a long, luxurious bath, I settled on the couch with a bowl of bolognese and a glass of wine, and flicked on the television. I couldn't remember the last time I'd gone full couch potato. Even those rare moments when I did find a little spare time, I usually felt like I shouldn't waste it on the likes of commercial television, but there's something to be said for just sitting down and zoning out occasionally.

I channel surfed for a while, flicking from one terrible reality show to the next. Even by my vegging out standards, most of the stuff was truly appalling.

At some point in my wandering I skipped to BBC News.

"—been nearly a week and police still don't know the motive behind the killing, but a source inside British parliament says it could have been politically motivated."

I froze. There was a picture of a shirtless man on the screen. He looked to be in his sixties, but was still fit, with a broad chest and thick arms that belied the wrinkles on his face. I'd never seen him before, but nonetheless there was one very familiar thing about him. Tattooed on his right bicep was a stylised letter A. The image was grainy and indistinct — it looked like a hasty camera phone holiday snap — but the mark appeared almost identical to the one Sebastian wore.

The shot cut to a police man. "Our initial findings indicate that Mister Reynolds was tortured, possibly for several days, before eventually dying of his injuries. We're working closely with the government in our investigation."

The program moved on to another story, but I was no longer paying attention. I'd never seen that symbol before meeting Sebastian. If the two of them had shared a different tattoo, a dragon or skull and crossbones or some other generic ink, I wouldn't have thought much of it, but this was a very specific image with very specific typography. It looked to be a different size, and was in a different place on his body, but still, it was a little eerie.

Firing up my laptop, I began looking for more information. The man's name was Christian Reynolds and he'd been the environment secretary of state for the British Government. He'd been a British citizen his whole life and a government employee for thirty years. No one knew for sure why he'd been killed, but based on the extensive torture he'd suffered, it was suspected to have been about information. I couldn't find a better picture of him, but after taking a closer look at the one shot that was circulating, I was fairly convinced that the marking was the same.

It had to be a coincidence. He and Sebastian were worlds apart. Different countries, different careers, different generations. Perhaps it was just a more common symbol than I realised.

I knew the smart thing to do was just forget about it. I'd caused enough trouble already by letting my paranoia get the better of me. What was I going to do? Wander up to Sebastian and say, "Excuse me, but do you happen know this random dead guy from the other side of the world?" It sounded absurd.

But as I flicked the television to another station and tried to focus on My Kitchen Rules, my mind continued to wander. Something about that ornate little symbol bothered me. I just couldn't put my finger on it.

Chapter 4

A few nights later I was once again out having drinks with the girls. My week had gone steadily downhill since Sebastian's call, and when Lou had suggested we hit the town, I'd jumped at the opportunity.

"Nothing says 'Friday Night' like a tray of Mojitos," I said, setting our drinks on the table.

"Hear hear," replied Ruth, raising her glass. She took a long sip and sighed appreciatively.

"So now that it's had a few weeks to sink in, how's it feel to be the future Mrs Steven Page, Lou?" I asked.

"No complaints. To be honest it's pretty much the same, but it makes Steve more comfortable. We want to start trying for kids soon, and his parents just wouldn't be able to stomach it if we didn't tie the knot first."

"Bah, kids, weddings, I don't like all this growing up," said Ruth. "Pretty soon I'll be sculling cheap vodka alone in Jackson's on a Friday night, while you two host dinner parties and play charades, or whatever the fuck it is responsible people do in their downtime. It's selfish, is what it is."

"Hey don't lump me in with that crowd," I said. "There are no nappies or white dresses in my future."

Lou grinned at me. "That's not what I hear. I hear you

might have a mystery gentleman of your own, now."

I shot Ruth a look.

"Hey, she dragged it out of me!"

I glared at her for a few seconds, but eventually broke into a laugh. I'm not sure what else I expected. Once you told Ruth something it was as good as front page news.

"It's not like that. It's strictly a casual thing," I told Lou.

"So? These things always start out casual. That's what the first few dates are. Doesn't mean it can't go somewhere eventually."

"With this guy, I think it does. He's not exactly the settling down type. I struggle to picture any woman keeping hold of him for very long. Besides, he's made his intentions perfectly clear, and I'm fine with that."

At that moment, my phone started buzzing in my bag with Sebastian's name flashing across the screen. "Speak of the devil," I said.

"He's back in town?" Ruth asked.

I shrugged. "Let's find out." I answered the call. "Hey."

"Sophia." The word sounded impossibly sweet off his tongue. He claimed he'd trained girls to come with a simple command, and the longer I knew him, the more I believed that might be true.

"Back in sunny Sydney?" I asked.

"Yes, I arrived this afternoon."

"Good flight?"

He laughed. "Flights are never good. Let's go with the word tolerable."

"Fair enough."

"I'd like to see you, Sophia. Tonight, if possible."

"Aww, did you miss me?"

"You don't know the half of it. I couldn't get the image of you playing with yourself out of my mind. I haven't been able to concentrate for days. I intend to make you do that again and this time I'm going to lick your pussy clean myself."

I blushed. There was something so hot about discussing such intimate things with my friends just a few feet away.

"I think I can arrange that," I said coyly.

"Excellent. There's a little company gathering I need to go to now. Nothing like the other week, a small group, but there are some people there I have to talk to. Why don't you come with me? We can have a drink, and after we can see about that show."

"I'm out with the girls at the moment," I said, although both of them were waving me on. "Also, I'm not dressed for a fancy party."

"How many times do I have to tell you that I don't care what you're wearing? You look gorgeous no matter what. Besides, if I have my way, you won't be wearing much of anything for very long. Will your friends mind if I steal you away?"

I glanced at their eager faces. "I think they'll cope," I said.

"Wonderful. Where are you?"

"Zeta bar, in the Hilton Hotel."

"I know it. I'll be there in half an hour."

"See you then."

Ruth snorted as I stashed my phone back in my purse. "Yeah, casual indeed."

"What?" I replied.

"Look at you, you can't wipe the dopey smile off your face."

"I can too!" I said, making a conscious effort to twist my mouth into a scowl. It was surprisingly difficult.

"Lou?" Ruth said, turning to the other woman.

She grinned at me. "If you'd been any more gooey-eyed, Soph, you'd have been melting onto the table."

I shifted uncomfortably in my seat. Sure, I was excited to see Sebastian, but that was purely my raging libido talking. "You can shut up, both of you. It's just fun because it's new, you know? That's all."

"If you say so," said Lou, although her expression said she didn't buy it.

"Anyway, he'll be here soon, so I'd appreciate if you two could do your best not to embarrass me."

I was secretly looking forward to them meeting Sebastian. I'm not ashamed to admit that I wanted to show him off a little. I'd been with attractive guys in the past, but none had nearly the same visceral impact that he did. His sheer presence and overt sexuality were a sight to behold. I couldn't wait to see the effect he'd have on the girls.

He didn't disappoint. A little while later, I spotted him sauntering through the crowd.

"So somehow she thinks it's my responsibility because..." Lou was saying to Ruth, however she trailed off as Sebastian appeared behind me.

"Sophia," he said, laying a hand gently on my shoulder.

"Right on time," I replied. "Sebastian, these are my friends, Ruth and Louisa."

"A pleasure to meet you," he said, shaking each of their hands. They returned the gesture dumbly, their mouths hanging slightly open like they'd forgotten how to speak. It was incredibly satisfying seeing them stilled like that, although I couldn't say that I blamed them. He looked good enough to eat. Somehow he'd managed to maintain that perfect level of rough stubble he'd worn the first night we met. That, combined with his wild black curls and roguish smile, gave him an exotic, devil may care look that practically screamed, "mind blowing orgasms!" I didn't think there was a woman in the room who would be immune to that.

"You too," said Ruth eventually. "Would you like to sit down? We could get another round."

"As much as I hate to turn down the company of three beautiful women, we should go. The party has already started. You two don't mind if I take her away do you? I'd be in your debt."

They both shook their heads slowly.

"Wonderful. I'm just going to get a glass of water and then we'll go, okay?"

"Sure," I replied.

I could only grin as their eyes followed him across the room.

"Jesus, Soph," said Lou, when he was out of earshot, "I take back what I said before. I think you'd be hard pressed not to go a little gooey with him on the other end of the line."

Ruth exhaled slowly. "Yeah, I've gotta hand it to you hon', that is one fine specimen of a man. I don't suppose he has any eligible friends?"

I laughed. "I'll let you know after I meet some of them tonight."

She turned to Lou. "Think you could find your way back to that bar? Maybe there's another function we can slip our way into. Something with firemen, hopefully."

"Give me another few drinks and I might just be on board," Lou replied. She grinned at Ruth's surprised expression. "What? I'm engaged, not dead. I can look!"

At that moment Sebastian returned. "Ready?"

I nodded. "Yep."

"You have a good night, girls," he said.

"You too," replied Lou.

Joe was waiting by the curb outside. "Hi Joe."

"Good evening, Sophia."

"What did you get up to while Sebastian was gone? Did

37

you go out and paint the town red?"

"Oh, nothing as exciting as that I'm afraid. It was a lot of staring at the phone and waiting for him to call, looking back wistfully on old pictures of me driving him around, that sort of thing."

Sebastian grinned. "That's what I like about you, Joe, that unwavering respect."

"I try, sir."

Joe opened the door and Sebastian ushered me through, easing in behind me. In a few moments the engine growled and we pulled out into the Sydney traffic. It was peak hour and the streets were thronging with cars. I never tire of that busyness. The first chance I got I moved from the suburbs to the city and never looked back. There's a living vibration to it, a sense of constant fluctuation that's a thrill to be a part of.

The back seats of the limo were spacious, with room for five or six to sit comfortably, but nonetheless Sebastian had guided me to one corner and then slid in next to me until our thighs were touching. I couldn't have moved even if I'd wanted to. Not that I did. I'd fantasised all week about being close to him, and now that I was, my body was kicking into overdrive. His raw presence radiated over me. There was an amazing sense of banked power to him. Even in the simple act of sitting in a car, he somehow looked primed, like a lion at rest between meals.

He looked over at me, something carnal flaring in his eyes. "Sophia," he said, and then taking my head in one hand and my shoulder in the other, he pulled me in, capturing my lips in his. Instantly, the heat simmering in my stomach began to boil over. This was what I'd been waiting for.

His kiss was hungry and fierce, an act of raw desire. He ran his hands through my hair, desperately pulling me closer, as though trying to fold the two of us into one. I loved that I stoked such passion in him. In that one simple gesture I could feel the weight of the week we'd been apart. He hadn't been lying. He'd been longing for me as much as I had him.

Our tongues darted together, exploring each other's mouths. I don't know why, but he tasted sweet, like strawberries and wood smoke. I quivered and sucked in a sharp breath as his fingers began to work their way up the soft flesh of my thighs, gradually peeling back my skirt. Meanwhile his other hand had slid down my neck and looped inside the shoulder strap of my dress.

"My god, you don't know how much I've been thinking about you," he said, breaking the kiss. "I don't think I can wait until after the party. I need to have you right now."

I cleared my throat. "Here?" I asked, nodding quickly out the window. The glass was shaded, but I was still incredibly aware of the shifting crowd and other cars visible all around us. Not to mention Joe. We were separated by the privacy window, but nonetheless he'd have to be a fool not to realise what was going on.

"Here," said Sebastian, his voice leaving no room for argument. And before I had time to protest, he wrapped both hands around my hips and spun me around on top of him.

As my legs slid into place around his, my sex came to rest on the bulge in his pants, and whatever resistance I'd felt instantly melted away. He was firm as stone, and he pressed against me with an urgency that was impossible to ignore. I could feel the heat of him radiating through our clothes, making me acutely aware of how little material separated him from being inside me. At that moment I no longer cared about Joe, or the masses of weary commuters just a few arm's lengths away. I wanted him to take me. I needed it.

And he responded. He gripped me roughly, grinding his cock against me while pulling me in for another kiss. The pressure was so intense, the stimulation so overwhelming, that I felt like I might come then and there. I let out a low moan, misting the window next to me with the warmth of my breath.

"You know, it was very generous of you to change the rules for me the other day," I said, "but I've got a secret to tell you." I ran my hands over him, playfully caressing his chest before pulling him in to whisper in his ear. "I never finished the job."

"You didn't?"

I shook my head. "I came close. My vibrator was out and ready to go. But at the last second I realised it just wouldn't be the same. I wanted to save it. I wanted it to be you."

He closed his eyes, a low rumble emanating from his throat. "That is so insanely hot. How is it you can be such a perfect sub with so little training?"

"I'm just that talented, I guess," I said with a grin.

He laughed. "Well then, I'd better not make you wait any longer."

Slipping the dress from my shoulders he pulled it down, allowing my breasts to fall out into the open. "My god you're beautiful."

And then he dove on me. Suddenly, his mouth seemed to be everywhere. I let out a gasp as his tongue began playing out an exquisite velvet pattern across my chest. He kissed and licked his way in slow circles, greedily sucking on my nipples and teasing with the barest brush of teeth. His stubble felt coarse against my skin, contrasting deliciously with the softness of his lips.

As he ravished me, his hands began to traverse further, weaving behind me to ruck up my skirt. He didn't waste any time. A moan of anticipation fell from my lips as he yanked aside my panties.

40

"Are you nice and wet for me?" he asked, that low silky voice ratcheting my excitement up even higher.

I nodded furiously. "I've been wet for you for weeks."

He let out a long breath. "I love it when you talk like that." With agonising slowness he slipped his hand underneath me and drew a single finger along my slickened opening. I shuddered in pleasure.

He brought his finger forward, the tip glistening with my juices. "You weren't kidding." He gave it a long, slow, tantalising lick. "And you're just as sweet as I remember. Later I'll have a proper taste, but I can't wait anymore. I need to fuck you."

I let out an affirmative grunt, not wanting to delay him one second more. I could feel the weeks of excitement burning wildly inside me.

Taking me by the hips once more, he hoisted me up, placing me on my knees next to him with my ass in the air. With panther grace he rose into a crouch and unfastened his belt, letting his pants fall to the floor. Seeing his cock in the flesh sent a bolt of desire rolling through me. I'd never wanted anything inside me so badly before.

Seizing me in a powerful grip, he dragged me across to him and plunged his shaft straight into my pussy, burying it all the way to the base in a single explosive thrust. He let out an animal cry.

The strength of that motion stung as my body madly adjusted to accommodate his girth, but I didn't care. The longing in his movements dwarfed everything else. That I inspired such lust in him set me soaring.

"God Sophia, you're so tight. You feel amazing."

"I'm tight because you're big," I said, my voice broken and quavering. His cock stretched me out like nothing I'd ever felt before. I moaned with the fullness of it, every muscle

41

cinching tight around him, savouring that exquisite pressure. He responded in kind, wrapping both powerful hands around my shoulders and yanking me closer, giving him more leverage to grind himself against me. He fucked me with the desperation and ferocity of a man with one day to live.

With other men I'd been with, sex had always been an act of giving; give your partner pleasure and receive it in return. With Sebastian, there was no give, only take. He wasn't giving me an orgasm, he was taking it from me, claiming it for himself, and he did it with a fervour that bordered on frightening. That intensity ignited something inside me, a kind of deep-seated passion I'd never known I was capable of.

I wasn't going to last long. The glow of my orgasm was already rising up inside me. My muscles clenched tighter still as my body began to stretch and tremble in anticipation.

"No, not yet," he said, his voice hoarse. Even as aroused as he was, he knew I was close. His awareness of my body was almost inhuman. "You were saving it for me, so I want to watch you as it happens."

With a grunt, he pulled free of me, leaving an aching emptiness between my legs. Seizing me by the thighs, he flipped me easily onto my back.

I gazed up at him, breathless and quivering. He'd shed his jacket, and sometime in the commotion several of his shirt buttons had come undone. Crouching there, half dressed and coated in sweat, he looked wild and impossibly beautiful. His cock jutted out from his body, slick and shining with my juices. It pulsed and twitched in the sex-heavy air.

He slid in close, pressing the swollen head gently against my cleft.

"Please," I moaned. "Please."

Leaning in close, he gazed at me with those spectacular eyes. "You've earned this." He pushed himself back into me and began rocking back and forward, reaching out with one hand to stroke my clit. "This is what you've been waiting for."

"Sebastian!" I cried, my body heaving as my climax took hold. I thought the phrase 'seeing stars' was just an expression, but as a week's worth of pent up desire exploded inside me, that's exactly what happened. The whole world seemed to shatter before my eyes. The strength of it was so overwhelming I was sure I was going to black out.

As my pleasure began to subside, his movements grew faster. What little control had been evident on his face fell away as he finally gave in to his own desires. The noises from his throat became more guttural, his thrusts longer and harder.

I was still sensitive from the intensity of what had just happened, but the promise of having him burst inside me was so enticing it barely registered. My body wanted more of him, as much as he could give.

After a few more seconds he shuddered and went rigid. Watching him come in such an intimate position was the most erotic thing I'd ever seen. The ferocious ecstasy on his face, the way his body flexed and corded, it was almost enough to send me over the top again.

"God, Sophia," he said, when it was over. "I don't know how you keep doing that to me."

"Doing what?"

"Making me lose control. I was planning on waiting, drawing it out, but the second I saw you, I got hard."

"You're still hard now," I said with a giggle.

"And you're still wet. Believe me, it's taking most of my control not to take you again right now."

I reached out and ran my hand softly up the length of his erection. "Why don't you?"

He closed his eyes and drew a deep breath. "I want you

to save some energy for later. I have plans for you, plans that won't be much good if I've already tired you out."

"I'm not sure I could ever get tired of having this inside me."

"If you don't stop being such a tease I'm going to be forced to turn you over my knee," he said, stroking my ass delicately.

I trembled, remembering the last time he'd spanked me. "Is that a promise?" I asked.

He stared at me for a second, then shook his head and chuckled.

We stayed in a dishevelled, half naked embrace for several minutes while the streets blurred past around us. I loved the feeling of his arms around me. It was protective, comfortable, safe.

Chapter 5

A few minutes later, the car pulled up outside a towering apartment building. It looked like a new development; all sleek curves and stark colours.

"Take those off," Sebastian said, nodding at my panties as we were making ourselves presentable. "I loved thinking about you walking around naked under your skirt for me the other day. I want to spend tonight knowing there's nothing between me and that beautiful pussy."

I loved the way his mind worked. Everything was a naughty adventure with him.

Smiling seductively, I slid them down my legs, letting them dangle from my toes. "Why don't you hang on to them for me?"

"I believe you already owe me one pair of your underwear," he replied.

"Think of this as a down payment then."

He laughed. "How can I argue with that?"

They disappeared into his pocket. He ran his eyes over my now naked sex. "God, this is going to drive me crazy."

I knew the feeling. Now I'd be conscious of the fact that I was naked for him all evening.

As he began fastening his buttons, my eyes fell upon his

tattoo once more. Despite my best efforts, I hadn't been able to stop thinking about the man on the news. I knew it was stupid, but I couldn't shake the feeling that there was something more to it. I couldn't ask Sebastian about it directly of course. That would be opening a whole other can of crazy. But that didn't mean I couldn't fish for a little info.

"You know, I've been thinking recently about getting a tattoo," I said.

"Oh yeah?"

"Yeah. I've been planning to for a few years. I mean, I like the idea of it, but I keep putting it off because I can't pick a design. It's going to be on my body forever, so I want it to be something I love."

"That's fair enough."

I glanced casually at his chest. "How'd you pick yours?"

He laughed and looked a little sheepish. "Honestly? It was just one of the pre-made ones they have in-store."

"Really? That doesn't seem like you."

"What can I say? I wasn't always the pinnacle of sound judgement that I am now. In retrospect, I wish I'd had your foresight, but at the time it just seemed like something fun to do."

His regret sounded genuine. *See, Sophia, just a coincidence. Now can you stop trying to ruin this for yourself and forget about it?*

We hopped out of the car. "Go and get some dinner, Joe," Sebastian said. "I'll call you when we're done."

"Of course, sir." He didn't display any hint of embarrassment at what had happened, but perhaps he was simply used to that kind of behaviour. *Business as usual.* That thought brought me back down to earth a bit.

With that same gentle pressure as before, Sebastian guided me into the lobby. A girl buzzed us through and we

46

took the lift up.

Much like Sebastian's apartment, this one was spacious, elegant, and masculine. The entire far wall was sheet glass from floor to ceiling, offering a stunning view out over Hyde Park, and it opened on hinges to one side, leading to a softly lit balcony, complete with its own outdoor bar. There were people milling everywhere, all dressed like they'd just committed a group robbery of the Harrods designer section. "Low key, hey?" I asked.

He grinned. "Do you *remember* the last party of ours you were at? It's all relative."

"Fair point." This certainly wasn't as overwhelming as that first night. More casual richness than unbridled decadence.

Several pairs of eyes turned to us as we entered.

"There he is," said an energetic looking man who broke off from a group near the door. Like most of the men in the room he was handsome and well groomed, with closely cropped golden hair and a strong jaw. In many other circumstances, I'd probably have found him attractive, but watching he and Sebastian shake hands just emphasised how gorgeous my date was. With him in the room, every other man was relegated to second fiddle.

"Thomas, sorry we're late. We had a little car trouble."

I blushed, suddenly very aware that less than ten minutes earlier I'd been having wild, rough, explosive sex in the middle of a crowded road. I ran a hand through my hair, making sure everything was in place. Could Thomas tell? Sebastian had fucked me so thoroughly it felt like it should be obvious.

"This is my friend, Sophia," Sebastian continued.

"Lovely to meet you," Thomas said, extending a hand.

"You too," I replied.

He clapped. "So, what are you two drinking?"

"I'll get something in a minute," said Sebastian, scanning the room. "I want to have a word with Gabriel. Do you mind?" He gave me an apologetic smile.

"It's fine, go play businessman." He nodded thanks, turned and disappeared into the crowd.

"Well, what about you, Sophia?" Thomas asked. "Drink?"

"I wouldn't say no to a glass of red."

"I have just the thing. Come with me."

I attracted more than a few appraising glances as we headed for the balcony. Although everyone appeared to be having a good time, there was a certain cattiness in the air that the men seemed largely oblivious to. I could see it in the girls' postures and smiles and the way they sized each other up when they thought nobody was looking. It was the same vibe I had felt that first night in the bar, that this was all a competition and they were fighting tooth and nail for the best position. Anyone new was a threat. It made me feel decidedly uncomfortable.

"So, you and Sebastian work together?" I asked, trying my best to distract myself.

He nodded. "Locky and I started at Fraiser around the same time."

I snorted. "Locky?" I couldn't imagine anyone addressing Sebastian like that. He didn't seem like the sort of man who people made nicknames for.

Thomas grinned. "Yeah, an old joke from way back when. He hates it, so I save it for special occasions. Use it well."

I laughed. "I'll do that."

I strolled over to the balcony edge while he poured the wine. "You have a beautiful place here. The view is amazing."

He came over to join me, two glasses in hand. "Thanks.

I've been lucky. Fraiser Capital has been good to me."

"It seems like it's been good to all of its staff," I replied, gazing around. "No offence, it's just all a bit surreal."

Thomas laughed. "Believe me, I know what you mean. You kind of just get numb to it after a while. To be honest I barely come out here anymore. I know it makes me look like an asshole, but at some point you just start taking it all for granted."

I decided that I liked him. His self-deprecating humour was refreshingly different from the sort of stuffy, self-important conversation I'd been expecting. He felt like the sort of guy who'd be more at home in a local bar than a ritzy penthouse apartment.

"I don't think you're an asshole," I replied. "It's just hard to get your head around, you know?"

He nodded. "I know. When I first started actually making real money, it took me a solid year to adjust. I spent the first six months living off spaghetti and toasted sandwiches like I always had. I couldn't believe that people lived like this. Sometimes I actually think it might all be too much. Then again," he held up his glass, "it does have its perks."

I took a sip of my own wine and swished it lightly in my mouth. It was delicious, a cavalcade of flavours I didn't have the vocabulary or palate to identify. I had to agree; I wouldn't be complaining.

"So you weren't born into all this?" I asked.

He laughed. "Hell no. I grew up in a shitty little two bedroom fibro house down on the outskirts of Melbourne. I never had more than a few hundred bucks to my name until I started at Fraiser."

"Sorry. I just kind of assumed this was an old money sort of crowd."

"Oh it is, for the most part. But a few of us worked our

way in from the ground up. Sebastian is one of them actually."

My eyes widened. "No way. Really?" Thomas nodded. "But he seems so... comfortable here. So in control."

"He's always been like that. But yeah, he comes from some little town in Europe somewhere."

"So how did he wind up here?"

Thomas shrugged. "Not sure exactly. Fraiser Capital is multinational. We've got branches all over the place, so I assume he got recruited by one of them, but beyond that I don't know. He doesn't talk much about his past. He's kind of a private guy."

I laughed. "I'd noticed. He's got the dark and mysterious thing down to a T."

Thomas studied me for a few seconds, his expression growing sober. "You haven't been with Sebastian long, have you?"

I shook my head. "We only met a little over a month ago."

"Right. Well, can I offer you a piece of advice?"

"Sure, I guess."

"Try not to get in too deep."

I shifted uncomfortably. "What do you mean by that?"

He sighed. "Look, I don't know what sort of relationship you have with him and I don't want to know. It's none of my business. I'm just saying, be careful. He's a great guy, but he's also not the sort who stays put for very long, if you catch my drift. You seem like a nice girl and I'd hate to see you get hurt."

He was the third person tonight who'd seemed to think that maybe my feelings for Sebastian ran a little stronger than a casual fling. It made me uneasy. I'd thought I had a fairly good grasp on what our relationship was, but now I was starting to question that.

50

"I can take care of myself," I replied, a little more force-fully than I'd intended.

He raised his hands defensively. "Hey, I don't doubt it."

At that moment, we were approached by another man. "Hiding all the beautiful women outside again, Thomas?" he said, with a friendly grin. He was incredibly young looking, with a smooth round face that barely seemed like it should be out of high school.

"How else am I meant to protect them from the likes of you?" replied Thomas.

The stranger gave a little laugh. "Hi, I'm Trey," he said, extending his hand.

"Sophia," I said.

"Lovely to meet you. Please don't tell me you're here with this lout."

"Actually," replied Thomas, "she came with Sebastian."

"Ah," said the other man. "Well that makes more sense."

"Trey here is another of our illustrious colleagues," continued Thomas. "He's what you might call the baby of the group."

Trey sighed good-naturedly and rolled his eyes. "I'm twenty six," he said to me. "Thomas here is just threatened by my youthful exuberance. He knows it's only a matter of time before he's the one answering to me."

"Yeah, that's definitely it," said Thomas.

"Does that mean you're his boss?" I asked, spotting a chance to learn a little about the company.

The two men shared a glance. "In a manner of speaking," said Thomas. "Fraiser has a pretty loose hierarchy. Most of the time everyone is working on their own projects and can pretty much do what they want, but when push comes to shove there's a certain order to how we operate. It helps keep the ship on course."

"Makes sense," I said with a nod. "Although it's funny, I can't really see Sebastian taking orders from anyone."

Thomas smiled wryly. "Most of the time he ends up giving the orders, even if he perhaps shouldn't"

"Now *that* I can see."

I felt a set of hands slide around my waist. "My ears were burning," said Sebastian. "And it's a good thing, too. I leave you alone for ten minutes and the vultures start circling." Again, there was something so personal, so possessive about the gesture. No wonder people suspected something more serious between us. It was easy to forget the nature of our relationship when he behaved like that.

Tilting my head to the side, he leaned in for a lingering kiss. I could almost feel the testosterone radiating from him. The message was clear: *mine*. These were his friends, but still he couldn't help laying claim to what was his. I don't know why, but I liked that masculine jealousy.

Trey cleared his throat. "Lovely to see you too, Sebastian."

"They're both being perfect gentlemen," I told him. "Are you done already?"

"No, not yet. There's one more person I need to talk with, but he's not here yet, so I came to see how you were doing."

"I'm fine. Just learning a little more about you, Locky," I said, not quite able to contain my grin.

Sebastian's lips tightened, before curling up ever so slightly. "I should have known better than to leave her with you, Thomas."

He raised his hands defensively. "Hey, it just came up okay?"

A man approached from inside. "Gentlemen. Any of you feel like losing a little cash? A seat just opened up in the game."

I shot Sebastian a questioning look.

"Most Fridays we run a small poker game," he said.

"I know a little about poker," I replied. "Can I watch you play?"

As a child I'd spent more than a few Friday nights watching my father and his buddies play cards. Games have always fascinated me. I love the challenge of working out how to beat an opponent within the confines of a specific set of rules. I think that's why I became a lawyer. When my dad realised how interested I was by it all, he took me aside and taught me how to play. Most of the time it was just the two of us, but occasionally he let me sit in with his friends. "The big game," he called it. Over time I learned to hold my own, although I hadn't played for years now.

Sebastian pondered for a second. "Sure, why not. Excuse us."

"Sure. Good luck," replied Thomas.

I leaned in to Sebastian's ear as we were led inside. "Your friends seem like fun. Perhaps I actually might be able to land Ruth a sexy venture capitalist of her own."

He chuckled. "You might be barking up the wrong trees there. Thomas works even harder than I do. He's a company man through and through. Relationships just get in the way, according to him. And Trey has been off the market for the last year or so."

"Pity. Oh well, the night is young. Plenty of time for me to play cupid."

He could only smile and shake his head.

We followed the other man across the lounge and through to an adjacent room. Inside was a group of men, chatting and laughing loudly around a large felt covered card table. The surface was littered with stacks of chips in varying size and colours.

"I should probably fold but... fuck it, I call," said one of the players, as we entered. He was an older man, and his strong features and heavy Scottish accent made me think of Sean Connery. "What have you got?"

The man he was speaking to stared for a few seconds before breaking into a rueful smile. "You've got me." He threw his cards towards the centre of the table.

"I knew it!" roared the Scot. "Don't try and cheat a cheater, Jack, you'll never get away with it!"

A few of the players noticed our presence. "Ah, Sebastian," said the one sitting nearest them, "come to try your luck? Someone needs to break Ewan's hot streak or we'll never hear the end of it." He nodded at the older man, who was now grinning and scooping in the pile of chips from the centre of the table.

"The more the merrier," replied Ewan. "His money's as good as anyone's." He spotted me for the first time. "Is this your secret weapon, Sebastian? Your own personal cheer squad?"

I opened my mouth to defend myself, but Sebastian got in first. "Settle down, Ewan. She just wants to watch." He turned to me. "Sorry, just try to ignore him," he whispered. "He gets like this when he's had a few."

I still felt like I should say something, but I didn't want to cause a scene, so I let it go. Taking my hand, Sebastian led me around the table to the spare seat. I pulled up a bar stool and sat behind him, my hands resting lightly on his shoulder.

"So, how much you in for, Sebastian?" asked the man who had greeted us.

Sebastian glanced around the table, sizing up the other player's stacks. "Five hundred I guess."

Several towers of chips were cut out and placed in front of him. It wasn't really what I was expecting. I'd had visions of bricks of hundred dollar bills being tossed around like dollar coins, but things seemed to be much more relaxed than that. It wasn't a small game by any stretch of the imagination — by my count some of them had several thousand dollars in front of them — but compared to the sort of wealth I knew they commanded, they were playing what amounted to penny stakes.

"Five hundred it is," said the dealer. "Shall we play?"

The game resumed. It took me all of two hands to work out that this wasn't an ordinary poker game. The action was fast and reckless; exactly what I'd expected from men playing stakes far below what they could afford. Almost every other hand ended with a huge pot. Often, that's the sign of a weak player, but as the game progressed, I began to see that they weren't playing badly at all. They had a kind of raw cunning to their style that made up for their lack of restraint.

Even during the lulls, I was enjoying being a fly on the wall. It was fascinating watching Sebastian with his colleagues. Seeing him laugh and joke along with the rest of the guys made him seem more human, somehow. He still had that steely intensity, but the camaraderie tempered it a little. It was a side of him I hadn't seen before.

Every so often he glanced back at me and smiled, making sure I wasn't bored. It was nice that just because he was with his friends he hadn't forgotten about me.

Ewan continued to drink and get more raucous, drawing more than a few uncomfortable looks from the other players.

"Why don't you guys just kick him out?" I asked Sebastian quietly.

He sighed. "You know that annoying uncle you don't really like, but are obligated to keep inviting? That's Ewan."

"My mum kicked *my* uncle out at Christmas last year for making a scene."

He laughed. "Somehow that doesn't surprise me. But be that as it may, we don't do things that way here. Our office is like a big family, and people don't get excluded."

A few hands later Sebastian got involved in a pot with a quiet, dark skinned man that everyone called Jav.

"Two fifty," Jav said, throwing some chips into the middle. It was a big bet. Big enough to be scary.

Sebastian sighed and checked his cards once more. His hand was weak. He'd been going for a flush and had missed, so he effectively had nothing at all.

I could tell he was about to throw his cards away, but I reached out and tapped his arm. "He's full of shit," I whispered. While the others had been chatting, I'd been paying close attention to the game, and had a pretty good feel for how everyone was playing.

"What?" Sebastian said.

I hesitated. I realised Sebastian might not appreciate me giving him advice. Also there was a chance I was wrong and would cost him a bunch of money. But my gut told me he was making a mistake, so I decided to bite the bullet. "Jav, he's full of shit. Remember a few hands ago when he bet small at the end with the straight? He likes to sucker you into a call when he's strong. He wouldn't bet this big if he had it. His hand missed as well. You should raise. He'll fold and you'll win the pot."

Sebastian studied me for a few seconds, a curious smile playing on his lips. "You're sure?"

I nodded slowly.

"Okay." He reached for a stack of chips. "Raise to five hundred," he announced.

Jav instantly threw his hand away. "All yours," he said.

"You know 'a little about poker' hey?" Sebastian said to me, as he raked in his winnings.

I grinned. "A little." It felt good to know I wasn't out-classed by these world-conquering men.

"I'll keep that in mind."

The game continued, and Sebastian gradually increased his stack. Soon, it was almost as big as Ewan's, with two towers of the green chips I'd worked out were fifties. It was an intimidating sum of money to be gambling with. Several more times during big hands Sebastian turned to me, seeking my advice about a particular decision. I don't know if he was just indulging me, or genuinely wanted my help, but it was nice to be included.

A few minutes later, one of the players left and was replaced by Trey.

"Gentlemen," he said.

"Well well well, if it isn't my favourite ATM," said one of the other men. "Time for your weekly donation, is it?"

"Not tonight my friend," replied Trey, "tonight is going to be my night. I can feel it."

The amused expressions that sprung up around the table said nobody really believed that.

"What's all that about?" I whispered to Sebastian.

He gave a little shake of his head. "Trey is just terrible at poker, that's all. And everybody knows it but him. At this point it's become a matter of pride more than logic, I think."

It only took a couple of hands for me to see that Sebastian was right. Trey was nothing short of awful, bluffing when he had no business bluffing and calling when presented with a clear fold. Mostly due to good luck he managed to win a little, but luck inevitably runs out in the end.

As one hand ended, a man who had been lingering by the door approached. "Sebastian, I hear you've been looking for me."

Sebastian nodded a greeting. "Will. About time you

showed up. Can we go and talk for a few minutes?"

"Sure."

He turned to me. "Want to hold down the fort while I'm gone?" he asked, gesturing to the table.

The huge wall of chips loomed up at me. "Oh I can't play with that kind of money."

"Sure you can. You've been doing just fine from back there. Why not take a turn in the hot seat?"

I waved him off. "Really, I wouldn't want to ruin all your hard work."

"If I thought you were likely to do that, I wouldn't ask. Look, either you play, or we lose our spot. It'll just be a few minutes, I promise."

I eyed the men around the table. As intimidating as the prospect of playing with them directly was, it was also kind of exciting. You don't get into law unless you have a healthy competitive streak. "Well, if it's just for a few hands..."

"Excellent." He got to his feet. "Everyone, Sophia here will take my place until I get back. Play nice with her." He winked at me. "Back in a few."

I slid into his seat.

"Not sure we've ever had a girl at this table," said Ewan, clearly not happy about the fact.

"It's kind of nice," said one of the other men. "Gives us something prettier to look at than your ugly mug." Laughter rippled through the room and Ewan scowled at me, although he kept silent.

Play resumed, and soon enough Trey found himself in a tight spot. All the cards had been dealt, and he was facing a massive final bet. I knew straight away his opponent had something strong. He had shown no propensity to bluff in spots like that. But Trey appeared oblivious. Rather than folding as he should, he seemed to be considering making a heroic call. Sure it would look amazing if he was right, but the chances of that seemed impossibly low.

Sure enough, after about thirty seconds, he pushed his chips into the middle. "Call." He wore a rather triumphant look, but it quickly dissipated as his opponent flipped over his cards.

"Full house," he said with a smirk.

Trey stared for a few seconds, before smashing a fist down on the table and throwing his hand away.

"Have you ever considered taking up knitting, Trey?" Jav asked. "Or maybe stamp collecting? There's not a lot of profit there, true, but at least you wouldn't be actively losing money."

Trey just stared down at his few remaining chips and shook his head. I felt bad for him, but there wasn't much I could do.

The game continued. I still hadn't played a hand. Part of me wanted to jump in and throw my chips around as recklessly as the rest of them, but I was afraid of putting Sebastian's stack at risk.

"Is that your plan then?" asked Ewan, after a few minutes of this. "Just play scared and fold until Sebastian gets back?"

Despite the fact that he was right, I was sick of his banter by that point. "I'm not scared. I'm just waiting for the right hand to take your money, that's all," I replied, as sweetly as possible.

There were several chuckles. "That sounds like a challenge to me, Ewan," said Jav.

"That it does," the other man replied, staring straight into my eyes. I knew that from that moment it was game on between us. The second I played a hand, he'd be all over me.

And a few minutes later, I was dealt something I couldn't

ignore. A pair of Queens. One of the best starting combinations possible. My pulse quickened. This was it.

I raised, and several people came along for the ride, including my new friend. The first three cards dealt into the centre looked harmless, so I bet again. Everyone folded until it got around to Ewan.

"Finally found some stones, hey?" he asked. "Alright then, let's play." He threw in enough chips to match my bet. Everyone else folded.

The next card didn't change much, but nonetheless I began to feel nervous. The first few bets in any given hand are relatively small, but as the money in the middle grows, so do the size of the wagers. There was already a large sum in the centre of the table. This hand had the potential to get out of control very quickly.

I considered just cutting my losses and giving up, but I couldn't stomach the thought of giving Ewan that satisfaction. I'd sat down to compete, and so compete I would. With shaking hands, I bet again.

He thought for about thirty seconds, staring me right in the eyes. "Okay," he said, then called once again.

The final card was an Ace. It wasn't very likely that it helped Ewan at all, but it was still a scary card. One of the only ones higher than my pair. I didn't think I could bet again.

"Check," I said, passing the action over to him.

Instantly he pushed a tall stack of greens into the centre. "Nine hundred."

I exhaled slowly. It was a huge bet; all of my remaining chips. My first instinct was to fold. I couldn't imagine calling such a bet and being wrong, and Ewan had made a habit out of betting big when he had the goods. For all his recklessness, he hadn't shown much of a propensity to bluff.

But as I thought it through, I couldn't shake the feeling that I was just being bullied. My presence clearly offended him, and this was the perfect opportunity for him to show me who was boss.

As if on cue, he spoke. "Just let it go, girl," he said. "You've still got most of your lad's money. There's no shame in admitting you're outgunned here."

I'm not sure if it was his tone or the smug look on his face that did it, but I suddenly knew I couldn't fold. If I was wrong, I was wrong, but I wasn't going to let him intimidate me.

With my heartbeat thundering in my ears, I silently pushed my money forwards and flipped up my hand.

He gazed at me for what felt like a lifetime, his mouth slowly twisting into a snarl, before shooting wordlessly to his feet and storming from the room. The table erupted into applause.

"I guess he folds," said Sebastian from behind me. I hadn't even realised he was back. "God, that was the most satisfying thing I've seen in a while."

I grinned. "It felt pretty damn satisfying too."

"You should bring her along more often, Sebastian," said Jav. "I can't remember the last time I enjoyed a show as much as that."

Sebastian grinned. "I told you you could handle it," he said to me.

"Oh I knew I could too, I just didn't want to embarrass your friends here."

He laughed. "That's very gracious of you."

I smiled. "After that hand though, I think it's time to call it a night. Not sure my heart can take much more." I started gathering up the chips. "Still, over a thousand bucks profit for a couple of hours work. Not a bad night."

"It was a little more than that."

I paused and did a quick count in my head. "Well, I guess it might be closer to one point five, if you add up all the change."

He stared at me for several seconds. "Sophia, that hand you just won was worth a little over two point two million dollars."

I did a double take. "Excuse me?"

"You didn't know?"

Something hot surged through me. "Know? How could I know?" I said, my voice getting progressively louder. "You said you were buying in for five hundred."

"Yes, five hundred thousand."

I looked down at the stack of chips once more, my eyes wide. There was more money in front of me than both my parents had made in their entire lives. I was no stranger to extravagance — the partners at work were notorious for their heinous disregard for money — but this took it to a whole new level. It seemed almost impossible to comprehend. "Holy shit. How the hell could you let me play with that kind of money? I could have lost it all!"

"But you didn't."

I shook my head slowly. "I know but still...fuck."

"Relax. You showed me you knew how to play. I had faith things would work out. And if they didn't, then c'est la vie. It's only money."

Several of the other players were watching this exchange with amusement. "He's lost more than that in a night before, Sophia," said Trey, who seemed to have recovered from his own loss. "And I dare say I'd take you over him if it were my money," he said with a wink.

Sebastian tried to look offended, but he couldn't quite hide his smile. He really did seem completely at ease with the situation. Perhaps he really would have been okay if I'd lost.

"Still," I said to him, "the next time you put me in charge of a million dollars, do me a favour and let me know, okay?"

"Of course. Sorry, I really thought you were aware. Anyway, look on the bright side. Since you're responsible for a large chunk of the winnings, you're entitled to a cut of the profits. How's fifty fifty sound?"

I gaped up at him. "I can't do that."

"Of course you can. You earned it."

"No, I didn't. I won it by accident, using your money, playing for stakes that I was totally unaware of."

"But you deserve some kind of reward. I want you to have it."

"Well I don't want it. It feels too much like a handout."

"Sophia—"

"—I'm not taking it, Sebastian! End of discussion."

Something in my tone must have got through to him, because his expression softened. "Okay. I'm sorry. I didn't mean to push."

I took a deep breath. "It's alright. I just don't do well with charity, you know? I like to earn my success."

He nodded slowly, a strange smile appearing on his face. "I completely respect that. Like I said, I'm sorry. Can we not let this ruin our night?" He leaned in so only I could hear his words. "I still have plans for you and I'd hate for them to go unfulfilled." As he spoke, he reached out and ran a hand tantalisingly down my hip.

I could already feel my tension ebbing away. It was difficult to be too angry at a man whose only crime was offering you half a million dollars. Especially if that man was a smoking hot sex god who wanted to take you home and do unspeakable things to you.

I sighed dramatically. "Fine. You know you're lucky

you're so damn sexy."

"Am I now?" he said with a laugh.

I tutted and shook my head. "Fake modesty doesn't suit you. Shall we go?"

"Sure." He signalled for someone to tally up his chips, explaining that the money would be wired to him later. We said our goodbyes and headed for the car.

He must have called Joe at some point, because the older man was waiting for us when we got downstairs.

"Good night, sir?" he asked, as he opened the door.

Sebastian nodded. "Yes, although I do believe it's about to get better."

I blushed, although I'm not sure why. Given that less than two hours ago we'd been having incredibly obvious sex not five feet away from Joe, it felt like the time for embarrassment had passed. We slid into the back cabin and the car took off.

Our lack of restraint on the earlier trip had left me sated, but that melted away almost as soon as the door closed behind us. Trapped with Sebastian in the privacy of the car, the air instantly seemed to grow warmer. It was like we couldn't be alone together without there being some kind of sexual charge.

He must have felt it too. Sliding closer, he leaned in and planted a soft kiss on the nape of my neck. "I can't wait to get you home," he whispered in my ear. "I believe I was promised a show."

"And I intend to give you one," I replied.

I reached for him, trying to pull him in for a kiss, but he caught my hands in his. "Uh uh. I lost control once tonight. I'm not going to do it again. I want to wait until I've got you exactly the way I want you."

The way he said that made my sex clench with anticipation.

We sat quietly for a minute, Sebastian staring thoughtfully out the window.

"Most girls would have taken the money," he said eventually.

"What?"

"Inside earlier, most girls I've dated would have taken the money."

"Well, I'm not like most girls."

I thought perhaps we were going to go round two over my refusal, but instead he just smiled ever so slightly. "No, you aren't." A few seconds passed. "You know, I think you left quite the impression on my friends."

"Oh yeah?"

"Ewan was right, I don't think there have been many women at that table. Not because they weren't wanted, it just doesn't really happen. But still, you handled yourself wonderfully. You didn't let them intimidate you."

I looked sheepish. "Would it shatter your impression of me if I said I was actually scared shitless?"

He laughed. "No. You might have been scared, but you went with your gut anyway and that's what matters. Fearless in the face of pressure. I can see now why you make a great lawyer."

I blushed and looked away. I didn't know why his praise meant so much to me, but it did. "Well, thanks. The pressure in law is usually a little different though. Mostly it's just pressure not to fall asleep in the middle of a document." I cleared my throat, hoping to change the subject. "Speaking of work, tell me about your trip."

He hesitated. I could almost feel that shield begin going up inside him. "Nothing to tell, really. I spent most of it in meetings."

"Come on, you can do better than that," I replied. I'd decided earlier in the day that I was going to try and get something out of him. I was still vaguely uncomfortable with how little I knew about his day to day life. It was like dating a secret agent. "Just give me generalities. You know a little about what I'm going through at work, I'd like to know the same."

He considered this, before eventually nodding. "I guess I can do generalities. In a nutshell, I'm working on a project. It's going to be a pretty big deal if it gets off the ground. A real revolution. But as with any progress, there are people who would rather it didn't happen."

"What, like competitors?" I asked.

"Exactly. Anyway, it's making things rather difficult for our clients."

"But surely that's their problem? Don't you just provide funding?"

"Yes and no. We've built up quite a few connections over the years, so if we can help clients in other ways, we do our best. Their success is our success."

"Right. So, I'm picturing a lot of secret lunch meetings and nondescript briefcases changing hands."

He laughed. "Sadly, it's not nearly that cool. Mostly it's just paperwork and boardrooms."

"Well, now it just sounds like my job."

Even though it was fairly mundane, I liked the fact that he'd given me something. I wasn't under any illusions that it meant much, but it was nice to feel like he trusted me, even if it was just a little.

Chapter 6

Soon we pulled up in front of his building. We said farewell to Joe and headed inside. As the lift rose to his apartment, Sebastian stepped around behind me, encasing me in his arms. His mouth found my ear, nibbling delicately. "Fuck, you don't know how difficult it was for me to get through those discussions earlier."

"Oh?" I asked, trying to sound innocent.

"All I could think about was that I had your panties in my pocket." His hand slid down my stomach, coming to rest provocatively close to my crotch. "You're naked under here for me right now."

"Naked and wet," I replied.

He growled softly. "We'll have to take care of that, won't we?"

The doors opened into his apartment. Without a word he took my hand and led me toward the bedroom, his movements radiating primal intent.

As we entered, he spun me lightly onto my back and then climbed on top of me. His mouth locked over mine, so sweet and so strong, and my body yielded beneath him. I'd never met a man whose kiss could break me so. Every stroke of his tongue seemed to echo through me all the way to my toes.

I felt his hands snaking across my skin and I responded in kind, enjoying the little moans and sharp breaths that I coaxed out of him as I explored his most intimate places. Under his shirt, his chest was warm and firm, and he still smelled lightly of sweat from our earlier exertions. I don't know why, but I liked that scent. It was so perfectly *him*.

We writhed together like that for some time, his fingers wandering, but never making any effort to remove my clothes. Eventually they found their way to my thighs and peeled up my skirt, my legs falling open without the slightest resistance. Every nerve in my body seemed to be standing on end. And this was just the beginning.

"I don't know why you were worried about your outfit," he said, pausing to study me. "You look hot as hell all corporate and sexed up."

"I'm glad you like it," I replied.

"I do. In fact, I don't want you to remove a thing. I want to watch you play with yourself right now."

I smiled seductively. "I think I can manage that."

He slid off the bed and sat on a nearby chair, his eyes never leaving my body. "Touch yourself for me, Sophia."

And I did as I was told. I was already impossibly excited. My finger glided with silken ease across my aching slit. I was tentative at first. Even given all that we'd shared, it was strangely invasive having someone else in the room while I pleasured myself. But as my passion mounted, my hesitance gradually fell away. I found the exhibitionism of performing intensely exciting. It was a different kind of intimacy. I was showing him something I'd never shown anyone before, something usually reserved just for me.

"Go slow," he said, barely able to drag his eyes away from my dancing fingers. "I want tonight to last."

I eased up, rubbing myself in gentle circles, savouring the

68

look of desire that burned on his face. There was a wonderful sense of power, seeing what my show was doing to him. The bulge in his pants was growing with every passing second.

I let out a soft moan as I brought my second hand down to play too, slipping it inside me while my first continued to focus on my clit.

"God, you look so fucking sexy like that," he said.

"I promised you a show didn't I?"

"You certainly did. I just have one suggestion."

"Oh?"

He reached out and opened a nearby chest of drawers, withdrawing a long, pale blue vibrator. It was thick and elegantly curved, with a smooth, rounded head and a small secondary arm about three quarters of the way down. "I bought it especially for you."

I took it from him, weighing it in my hand. It was larger than the one I had at home, almost as large as Sebastian's cock. A few weeks earlier I'd probably have said it was too big, but recent experience had taught me that I didn't know my limits as well as I thought.

"It's lovely." I said.

"It will look even more lovely inside you."

Taking the hint I flicked the switch to the lowest setting and the toy buzzed to life. My pussy was already wonderfully slick and the smooth rubber slid in easily. "Oh god," I groaned, as the head found my G-spot, sending a steady stream of pleasure rolling through me.

"That's it," he said. "Feels good, doesn't it?"

"God yes," I breathed.

With a little experimentation, I found the right angle to let the smaller arm work my clitoris at the same time. The simultaneous stimulation was exquisite.

"Now imagine how good it's going to feel when it's my

cock inside you instead."

"So get over here and fuck me!"

"Patience. Like I said, I want to draw it out. I will, however, give you a preview."

Reaching down, he unfastened his zipper, freeing his shaft from his pants. The sight of it made my whole body throb. Although I hadn't laid a finger on him, he was stiff as iron.

With tantalising slowness, he began to stroke himself, gripping the base firmly in his fist and working up and down. I'd never watched a man masturbate before. It had never seemed particularly appealing when we could be doing other things, but just a few moments with Sebastian showed me how wrong I'd been. This was off-the-charts hot, and made hotter by the fact that it was my body he was staring at. With every flick of his wrist, his cock seemed to swell just a little more.

"Don't stop," he said, and I realised that I had. The sight was so captivating that I'd forgotten my own pleasure. "But remember, you have to restrain yourself. If you come before I say so, there will be repercussions."

I resumed, now acutely aware of how close I was to the edge. I was doing my best to restrain myself, but the whole experience was so sensual that I didn't know if I could hold back. Our passions seemed to feed off one another, and as his pleasure mounted, so did my own. I loved staring into his eyes, watching him react as I performed for him, knowing that I was having the same effect on him. We weren't touching at all, but nonetheless there was a sense of connection to the situation that rivalled anything else I'd shared with him.

Our rhythms synchronised. As he stroked up, I thrust in. With every passing moment, my longing to have the real thing inside me grew. I burned for it. Despite the distance between us, in my head he was already buried eight inches deep, unravelling me with that tender ferocity as only he could.

Soon, I couldn't take any more. The charge pulsing between my legs threatened to overwhelm me. "I'm close."

His eyes narrowed. "Did I say you could come?"

"Please," I moaned, shifting the vibrator restlessly. I tried to move it to a less direct angle, but every part of me was humming by now, begging for release. "Please."

"Take out the vibrator, Sophia." The sudden sharpness in his voice caused me to slow. It was the same deep tone he'd used with Hannah the first night we'd met, that heavy command that seemed to echo right through me. Impossible to resist.

Mustering a mammoth amount of self-control, I withdrew the toy, my pussy clenching in protest.

"Better." He got to his feet and slid onto the bed and pinned my arms behind my head, capturing me beneath him. Leaning down, he planted several soft kisses along my neck. "Thank you for the show," he murmured into my ear. "It was wonderful, but now I think I want to take over."

"I think I'd like that," I replied.

Leaving one hand gripping my wrists, he brought the other down and wrapped it around his cock once more, guiding it between my legs until it was just an inch from entering me. "Is this what you want?"

"Yes." It took all my restraint not to take matters into my own hands and push myself onto him.

"You'll have to do better than that," he replied, easing his length closer still until the crown was resting softly against my lips. "Ask for it," he continued.

"Please, I want your cock. I want you to fuck me." The words came without the slightest hesitation. He had rendered me utterly shameless with desire.

He began to rub himself up and down, dipping towards my opening, before climbing again to tease my swollen trigger. The sensation was exquisite, almost to the point of pain; perfectly measured to tease, but never summon my release. I let out a strangled cry, a kind of desperate plea that came from deep down inside me where there were no words.

"I'll give you what you want, Sophia. I'll fuck you until you don't remember your own name." He brought his hand up to brush my cheek, staring down into my eyes. "But not just yet."

Before I realised what was happening, his hands slipped under the pillow, and something cold and metallic clicked into place around my wrists. I let out a surprised squeak. I'd known handcuffs were probably going to be part of the deal at some point, but nonetheless the sensation was a little frightening. These weren't your stereotypical fluffy, pink, 'I'm a kinky housewife' restraints. These were the real deal. There was no give, no softness or sensuality, just the implacable strength of steel.

Rather than simply pinning my arms in place, this time my bonds were linked to the bed frame. Not only was I restricted from using my hands, I couldn't escape, even if left alone. He had me at his mercy for as long as he desired.

To my credit, I managed to keep my mouth shut. I'd come to realise that surprises were just part of the experience with Sebastian. I simply had to trust that he'd never take me too far too fast.

"Perfect," he said, leaning backwards to admire his handiwork. "Now you're completely mine." His hands began to unfasten my buttons, chased by his mouth, licking and teasing the freshly exposed skin. Shock had temporarily sent my arousal scurrying to the back of my head, but the moment his lips touched me, it began pushing its way to the front again.

"This is mine," he said, planting a soft kiss across the centre of my belly. "And this," he continued, brushing his lips along the curve of my hips.

My shirt fell open, and he paused, savouring the sight of my lingerie. Thanks to my newfound obsession with sexy underwear, the bra I was wearing was rather low cut, and while the handcuffs prevented him from unfastening it completely, it didn't take more than a soft tug to pull the cups down slightly, exposing my hardened nipples. "And these are definitely mine," he said, taking one into his mouth and teasing the peak with his tongue.

I desperately wanted to reach out and push his head between my legs, but of course I couldn't. He could take as much time as he wanted. And he took ample advantage.

With agonising slowness he continued to work his way around my body, seemingly intent on leaving no stone untouched. He was a master of his craft, steadily stoking the fire inside me, but never letting it flare too much. I writhed against him, pleading for the climax that lay just out of reach, but he simply smiled. "This is what it is to submit, Sophia," he said. "To put your pleasure in the hands of another and trust that they'll take care of you." I had no answer for that. As maddening as it was, I knew he was right.

The exquisite foreplay continued. I lost all track of time. Soon, every inch of my skin was flushed and tingling. He was clearly enjoying watching me come undone. I started to think maybe he was never going to let me come, that he'd leave me chained there all night, a squirming, flustered wreck. But finally his kisses began to hone in on the soft flesh of my inner thighs.

"Please," I cried again, sensing that this was the time.

"Please what?" he asked.

"Please eat my pussy. Please make me come."

73

"Do you think you've earned it?"

I nodded vigorously. "I have."

He paused, and for a few dreadful seconds I thought I'd been mistaken. "I think so too," he said at last, and with a soft growl, he planted a long, slow kiss on my sex. I gasped. His tongue parted my aching folds, caressing me with strokes that managed to be strong and demanding, yet soft as a cloud. I rocked against him, the metal rim of the cuffs biting into my skin, yet the pain went all but unnoticed.

"Yes, yes," I moaned. "Keep going."

Most of the work had already been done. My body felt ready to burst. My hips began bucking, gyrating wildly as the pleasure cascading through me reached its crescendo. "Sebastian, I'm coming!"

With expert dexterity he guided me over the edge, milking every ounce of pleasure from my body, until I sunk, panting, into the bed.

He gazed at me for several seconds, radiating satisfaction. "That's the first of many tonight. I'm not done with you yet."

"I suspected that might be the case," I said weakly.

His cock flexed invitingly. As I stared at it, I knew what I wanted to do next. I needed to taste him like he'd tasted me. "But first, there's something I'd like to do to you," I continued, giving my lips a slow lick.

He let out a short laugh. "Oh? And what might that be?"

"Take off your clothes and I'll show you."

Smiling in amusement at the role reversal, he did as he was told, stripping away his suit until he stood naked before me. The sight of that lithe form caused my body to stir once more.

"Much better. Now come here and uncuff me. I want to suck your cock." Two months ago, I'd have laughed if anyone told me I'd be saying something so bold to a partner, but with

Sebastian, the old Sophia was nowhere in sight.

In moments he was just inches from my face, but he didn't reach for my restraints. "I'll let you give the orders this once," he said, "but we're still playing by my rules. The cuffs stay."

Well, that would be a new experience. But I'd never been one to shy away from a challenge. Shifting my position, I leaned forward and wrapped my lips around his swollen crown.

He exhaled slowly. "Oh Christ, that feels wonderful."

He tasted fantastic; warm, musky, and slightly salty. The width of him filled my mouth. I worked my lips slowly up and down, paying special attention to the soft track of skin just below the head, while my tongue swirled an intricate pattern across the underside of his shaft. It was an incredibly submissive position to be in, splayed below him, gazing up at his body while I pleasured him. He'd spent so long focused on me, I loved that I could give him the same in return.

"Lick it," he said, sliding free, and I did as ordered, lavishing him with slow strokes all the way to the root, then darting up to engulf him once more. Being bound changed the experience dramatically. I longed to reach out and seize the base in my fist, to pump it while I sucked him, but that wasn't an option. Instead, I focused on swallowing as much of him as I could.

"Yes, that's it, take it deeper," he said, seizing my head in his hands and guiding his length further down my throat. I drew a sharp breath through my nose, certain I was about to gag, but again he proved he was perfectly in tune with my body, never taking me over my limits. Gradually, he took over. I'd enjoyed being in control of his pleasure, but there was something erotic about having him fuck my mouth too. It was base, it was possessive, and it was hot as hell watching his self-control unravel before my eyes.

His fingers clenched tight around my hair as his strokes grew wilder. Our mutual masturbation had clearly taken a toll. He was close. I could feel each individual vein shift and pulse against my tongue. "Oh fuck, I'm going to come so hard," he groaned, and with several more mighty drives his body stiffened, and warmth exploded down my throat. His semen was sweet and salty and oh so good, and I swallowed every drop.

As he pulled free, I stared up at him, licking my lips once more for effect.

He shook his head and smiled. "God you're sexy." Leaning down, he locked his mouth over mine. "And extremely talented, if you don't mind me saying."

I grinned. "Not at all."

"I'm going to uncuff you now," he said, seizing my restraints. "I want you on all fours for what comes next."

"Next?" I asked.

He looked at me like I'd forgotten something incredibly obvious. "I still want to fuck you, Sophia."

"Don't you want a break or something?"

"Do I look like I need a break?" he asked, nodding to his cock. It was still rock hard and glistening with my saliva.

"Well, that's enough to offend a girl."

He laughed. "Don't be. It's a compliment. You drive me crazy. I seem to be hard all the time, since I met you."

His words stoked my arousal. "Well, it would be a shame not to take advantage of that."

"My thoughts exactly."

With barely concealed urgency, he flipped me onto my knees and slammed into me. I let out a long moan and rocked against him, revelling in the sensation of finally having him inside me.

"Fuck, I love how ready you are for me," he said.

I couldn't muster a reply. His body was thrumming, his strokes slow and purposeful, and they echoed through me in great waves. Wrapping his hands around my hips he yanked my body against his, burying himself in me as deeply as he could. The air was soon thick with our grunts and cries.

I'd been expecting my pleasure to build slowly, but it wasn't long before I could feel myself cresting again, helpless against that exquisite rhythm.

"Have you been wearing your butt plug like I asked?" Sebastian said, his fingers firmly squeezing my ass.

"Yes," I whispered, although the implication was lost on me. All I could focus on was the swelling inside me. A few more moments and I would be past the point of no return.

He slipped one hand underneath me, stroking my moistened lips with his thumb, coating it with my juices. "Then you might want to hold on."

That got my attention. But before I could voice a question, I felt a firm pressure against my rosette as he pushed his way in, and then all capacity for speech instantly fled.

I'd had no idea a finger there could feel so good. It magnified everything else he was doing to me a hundred times over. Something broke inside me, and my knuckles curled white around the bed sheets. I'd never come like that before. Not even with him. It felt like every individual cell in my body was rupturing all at once.

It was the kind of orgasm that should have left me in a crumpled heap, but Sebastian didn't stop, he didn't even slow, he just kept thrusting as my body clenched and buckled beneath him.

"More, Sophia. I need more. I'd make you come all night if I could."

And somehow, my body responded. With him, I felt like

perhaps I *could* go all night. The raw physical connection between us drowned out everything else.

Seizing my hips he flipped me around onto my back and lifted my legs to rest on his shoulder, squeezing my pussy even tighter around his hardness. With great drives he began fucking me once more, the new angle striking some long forgotten spot deep inside me. I could feel every inch of him, hot and rigid, as he urged my body towards another climax.

This one was different, less intense, but longer, and I yelled wordlessly as he brought me over the cusp.

"One more," he said, letting my legs drop back to the bed. The fire in his eyes made him look like a man possessed.

I winced. "Sebastian I can't. I can't."

"One more," he repeated.

With my legs free he altered positions again, leaning down and wrapping one arm behind my neck, locking us in a lover's embrace. His mouth found mine, grazing softly across my lips, before moving down my neck to flit gently across my nipples. His thrusts became soft, almost delicate, as he gradually coaxed my spent body back to life.

The intimacy of it all threatened to unravel me. We'd gone from kinky domination to tender lovemaking in just a few short minutes. I didn't understand. It was the kind of sex I expected to have with a lover of several years, not a self-professed anti-romantic playboy like Sebastian.

Christ Sophia, don't read too much into it. Can't you just enjoy a good thing for what it is?

But as we climaxed one final time together, clawing desperately at each other's bodies and choking out each other's names, I felt a wave of contentment unlike anything I'd experienced before.

Yeah, you might be in trouble here, girl.

Chapter 7

The whole next day, my conversation with Thomas played through my mind. In light of the things I'd felt last night, it was getting harder and harder to convince myself it was just sex with Sebastian. Our previous times together had been eye-opening, but this had been something more, something intimate. It filled a space inside me that I hadn't even known existed.

But there was no future there. Thomas had said it, as had Sebastian himself. Whatever I felt from him had to be my imagination. Letting myself think otherwise was a recipe for more heartbreak. And so I knuckled down and tried to concentrate on work.

A few mornings later, I received what appeared to be good news. In amongst the usual drudgery of my inbox was a request from Ernest to do some work on the Wrights case.

Hope this is more like what you were looking for. Enjoy!

I grinned. He'd come through after all! It was an important task too; hunting through client testimony and trying to distil it down to its core points. It was this sort of stuff that our case was built on. *High five, Sophia!*

Working as fast as I could, I ploughed through my other tasks. I figured I'd have them all done by midday, then I could spend the afternoon on the meaningful stuff. I should have realised that it was too good to be true.

At eleven thirty, I received an email from Jennifer.

Hey Soph.

Hope you're feeling better. Those prawns can be nasty things.

Need you to take care of something. This came down from Mr Bell himself and Alan asked that I get our best people on it, so naturally I thought of you. It needs to be taken care of ASAP. Have fun.

Attached was a series of case files for some tiny corporate litigation we were handling, with a note telling me to sift through and check for errors. It was lengthy, painstaking work, the kind most lawyers dread. To make matters worse, it took me all of a few seconds to see that the case wouldn't even make it to trial. There was barely enough evidence to make an accusation, let alone get a favourable judgement. She couldn't have crafted a more colossal waste of my time if she'd tried.

Although Ernest technically outranked her, Jennifer had invoked both Mr Bell's and Alan's names, which should have pushed it to the top of my pile. I doubted either of them had really laid eyes on it, but proving that would be annoying, time consuming, and probably fruitless.

I closed my eyes and attempted to contain my rage. It was impossible that it was mere coincidence. I finally received some real work, and out of the blue Jennifer miraculously conjured some mindless task for me. Not to mention her sickening faux chummy tone. She might as well have written "ha-hahaha" at the end of the email.

Before I knew what I was doing, I'd left my office and was storming across the floor to hers. Telling off a superior wasn't the smartest career move, but at that moment I didn't really care.

"Really?" I said, striding into her office unannounced.

"Sophia," she replied, smiling up at me like that was the most normal greeting in the world. "What a pleasure. Is everything okay?"

"What do you think? I've just been assigned work for the most pointless case on our books."

Somehow she managed to look perfectly innocent. "Oh?"

I glared at her. "The Phaidan File?"

"Oh that. Come on, you're being a bit dramatic don't you think? If anything it's a compliment. We needed someone with a good eye for detail, so I assigned you."

I felt my hands contract involuntarily into fists. I was a hair's breadth away from leaping over the desk and rearranging the details of her face. "It's bullshit, is what it is. That case is never going to see the inside of a court room and you know it."

"Oh I don't know about that. In any case, I'm just doing what I'm told."

"Oh yeah?" I said. "Well I'm not. I'm not wasting my afternoon on that crap when there's real work to be done."

She stared at me for several seconds, a calculating glint in her eyes. Eventually she shrugged. "Well, suit yourself. Obviously I can't force you." Her voice turned sweet. "I just hope nobody upstairs hears that you're rejecting assigned work. You know how this place is; it's a slippery slope to the bottom."

At that point I knew I'd played right into her hands. This was exactly the sort of reaction she'd been hoping for. It probably wasn't enough to land me in serious trouble, but causing me any kind of grief seemed to be a win in her books. She loved watching me squirm.

"Why, Jennifer?" I asked, hating myself for sounding so defeated.

For a moment a look of unrestrained glee spread over her face, but it was gone again in an instant. She was too smart to give up the game so easily. "Why what, Sophia?" she replied, her tone perfectly neutral.

Unable to stand another second in her presence, I spun and fled back to my office. Slamming the door behind me, I sat down and let out a long breath. *Calm blue ocean, Sophia.*

As much as Jennifer's antics angered me, I didn't know what I could do about them. The hierarchy was everything in our office, and despite how little she deserved it, she outranked me. That made her basically untouchable. Sure, I could try going to the higher ups, but it was career suicide to go behind a superior's back unless the problem was really serious. Once you had a reputation as a backstabber, nobody wanted to work with you. All I could really do was hunker down and try to roll with the punches.

I considered just giving in and doing the work she'd assigned, but try as I might, I couldn't make myself start it. Either way she was going to win. At least by refusing I kept some shred of dignity. I doubted she'd actually be petty enough to take it up the ladder, and if she did, well, it would probably only be a slap on the wrist.

So, gritting my teeth, I opened the Wrights files and began to work.

Chapter 8

Despite my best efforts to stay positive, Jennifer's meddling sent my mood plummeting. Even though she hadn't actually stopped me from working on Wrights, she'd soured the experience for me. Suddenly it felt like the wrong thing to do. I hated her for that.

To make matters worse, I kept running into her around the office. At first I thought it was just chance, but soon I realised she was doing it on purpose. She never said anything about our altercation, but the smarmy little smiles she shot me told me all I needed to know. She'd enjoyed her little prank immensely.

After two days of feeling like shit, I found myself reaching for the phone. I wasn't sure if emotional support fell under the terms of my relationship with Sebastian, but he was the first person I thought to call. There was something about his presence that made me feel comfortable and protected, and right now that was exactly what I needed.

He answered after five or six rings. "Sophia."

"Hey," I replied, trying my best to sound less morose than I felt. It didn't work.

"Is everything okay?" he asked.

I sighed. "Not really. Having a pretty rough few days actually."

"Oh, I'm sorry. Work stuff?"

"Yeah. Any chance you're free tonight? I could use some cheering up."

He hesitated. "I don't know, I've got a lot to do here."

"Just for a little while? I'd really like to see you. I'll even come to you."

There was another pause. "I guess I can spare an hour or two. Is ten okay?"

"Totally fine. I'll see you then."

Knowing I was seeing him later made the day a little more bearable.

He greeted me at the door when I arrived, looking as fresh as if he'd just woken up. Despite the late hour, he was still wearing a suit, although the tie was missing. Perhaps that was as far as 'casual' went for him.

"Hey," he said softly, pulling me in for a hug.

I stood there for a few moments enjoying the feel of his arms. "Hey," I replied eventually.

He led me inside.

"Thanks for making time," I said, once we were seated in the lounge room. "I know you're busy. I just really needed a friendly face."

He gave a dismissive wave. "Don't worry about it. I didn't like the way you sounded on the phone. So what's wrong?"

I sighed. Now that I actually had to explain it, it all felt a little petty, but there was no backing out now. I told him about what had happened.

He listened patiently, compassion evident on his face. He seemed genuinely troubled that I was upset.

"You think Jennifer is the reason you've been having so much trouble lately?" he asked, when I was done.

I shrugged. "I don't know. I doubt it. I mean, she's just a senior associate, not a partner. She doesn't have that kind of authority. Don't get me wrong, I'm sure it doesn't help and she probably takes every opportunity to talk me down when she can — in the sweetest way possible of course — but at the moment she seems content to just fuck with me instead."

"And you can't take it up the ladder at all? Surely that's office harassment or something."

"It wouldn't do any good. She's kissed the ass of every bigger paycheck in the company. All I'd do is make more trouble for myself."

He frowned. "So what are you going to do?"

I exhaled sharply. "I don't know. Either way I lose. I basically have to make a choice; the work I want to do, or the work I should do. It's so unfair." Those last words came out as a kind of high pitched squeal, and I suddenly realised how I was coming across. "God, I've turned into a whiny high-school girl. I'm sorry."

He smiled and reached out to stroke my knee. "It's okay. Seems to me it might be justified. Why does this woman dislike you so much?"

"I don't know. She seems to dislike most other women around the office. You'd think she'd want to stick together, but I get the sense she'd be happier if she were the only one. Plus, I think it pissed her off the way tasks got distributed when we both first started. Despite her position, she's just not really that good at her job, and it showed in her work. She got stuck doing the things I'm doing now, while I was working on the good stuff. It was only once she got her claws into the higher ups that she managed to drag herself out."

"Well, she sounds like a petty bitch."

Those words brought a smile to my face. I hadn't expected to hear Sebastian say something so catty. "That's a fairly accurate assessment." I shook my head. "I don't know, maybe I'm making too big of a deal out of it. Sometimes it just kind of feels like the whole place is conspiring against me, you know? I have no idea how long this Wrights work from Ernest is going to last. I suspect he had to fight pretty hard to get me assigned."

"Well, at least you've got someone on your side."

"That's true."

"You deserve better than this, Sophia."

"Thanks."

He slid closer on the couch and looped his arm around me. "I just wish there was something I could do."

"You've done plenty by just listening. I wasn't expecting any solutions, just someone to vent to."

He nodded but didn't reply.

We sat like that for a few minutes. It felt good to be snuggled against him. I hadn't been sure what to expect from this encounter, but he'd been incredibly kind and understanding. He'd even joined me in a little therapeutic spitefulness.

I leaned up and kissed him. It was meant to be just a short tender gesture, a thank you for being there for me, but whatever explosive chemistry our bodies shared seemed oblivious to any sort of context. In a matter of moments, our kiss deepened, his tongue entwining with mine while his hands found my neck. I felt something stirring inside my stomach, the first pleasant thing I'd felt since my encounter with Jennifer.

I broke away. "You know, I believe I was promised cheering up. I'm certainly feeling a little better, but I wouldn't describe myself as cheerful yet."

His expression turned sly. "Is that so? Well then, I still have work to do." Wrapping his hands around my thighs he lifted me on top of him.

As his lips began to trace their way down my shoulder, I

threw back my head, closed my eyes, and gave myself over to him. My body bowed and shuddered as he teased the spark inside me into a raging fire, one exquisite kiss at a time. His fingers wound towards to my buttons and began to work their way down, unwrapping me with torturous slowness.

The intimacy of the position filled me with warmth and security. The trust I had in moments like those made me feel so safe, so protected. In his hands, I could simply lose myself in the moment, utterly confident that whatever we were doing, he'd take care of me.

Slipping my blouse to one side and snapping my bra free with one deft flick of his wrist, he freed my breasts. He leaned backwards momentarily, gazing at my body with a heat so intense I was surprise I didn't burst into flames. "Has anyone ever told you how fucking perfect you are?"

I couldn't help but smile. "Not in those exact words."

"Then all the men you've ever met are idiots."

He resumed his maddening exploration. My nipples were hard peaks, begging for his mouth, and he obliged, grazing them softly with his tongue in a way that made my whole body contort. I curled my fingers through his hair, savouring the silky texture of it as he roved across my chest.

"Stand up, Sophia," he said.

I did as I was told. His eyes heavy with purpose, he reached around and unfastened the zipper of my skirt. With slow reverence he pulled it down, his breath stalling as my legs slowly came into view. Nobody had ever made me feel that way before; so utterly worshipped.

My panties came down next, and his pants followed, and then I was straddling him once more. I could feel the rigid heat of him radiating between my legs even before he entered me. His eyes widened as he gradually pushed his way past my folds, my body welcoming that sweet invasion with trembling hunger.

Reaching out, he wrapped one hand around my waist and the other around my shoulder, and began to guide me up and down. His grip was firm, but his motions remained slow and measured. I had no idea how a man could be so strong, so powerful, and yet so tender. I knew the animal was still locked away inside him somewhere, but this was exactly what I wanted right now, to make love, not to fuck, and so that's what he gave me.

I'd never been on top with him before. I liked the sensation of riding him, the way I could subtly shift my hips to change the angle of our motion. But even with me in such a position of strength, he was definitely still running the show. With firm pressure, he rocked my body against his, sheathing himself completely and grinding my clit against his pubic bone with a rhythm that set my whole body cresting.

"Oh Christ, don't stop," I moaned.

He reached up with one hand to caress my breasts, while leaning in and planting a string of hungry kisses along my collar bone. "I won't. I've got you, Sophia."

As I pressed my face into his hair, the scent of him washed over me, that perfect masculine potency. Nothing else had ever smelled that good.

"Are you going to come for me?" he asked, his voice full of warmth.

"Yes," I breathed, the pressure inside me swelling and rippling, following his command. Maintaining the same tantalising pace, he guided me over the edge, pulling me in close and sealing his mouth over mine as my release took hold. It wasn't the most powerful orgasm he'd given me, but it was the most affectionate, which at that moment made it utterly perfect.

He came wordlessly about twenty seconds later, his body

quivering beneath me. The whole time, he never broke that kiss.

"Well, consider me cheerful," I said, as we lay there afterwards.

He pulled me close. "I aim to please."

There was a wonderful sense of protection being encased between those arms. My troubles were still lurking in the back of my head somewhere, but I'd turned down the volume as best I could. I'd come to Sebastian to make me feel better, and he'd done an amazing job. Now I just wanted to enjoy that sensation for as long as possible.

Chapter 9

The following morning I woke to an empty bed, but it was not my own. It was the first time Sebastian and I had spent a full night together. Joe had always driven me home in the past. I didn't know if my staying over was intentional or not, but I chose to believe it was.

When I finally managed to drag myself from Sebastian's impossibly soft sheets, I found a folded white robe waiting for me on the dresser. It was accompanied by a note.

Your clothes were positively filthy, so I had them put in the wash. Your underwear too. They're drying at the moment, so you'll have to make do with something else for now.

I held it up in front of the mirror. Sheer and short, with a hem that barely covered the middle of my thighs, it hardly deserved the name 'robe' at all. I had no idea where he'd gotten it from.

My clothes may have had a day's wear, but "positively filthy" was definitely a stretch. It didn't take a rocket scientist to see that this was another of his little games. And as much as I enjoyed playing them, I felt a sudden desire to turn the tables on him.

A few minutes of exploring his extensive wardrobe turned up an over-sized tie-dyed tee shirt that fell all the way to my knees. It wasn't the sort of thing I could ever see Sebastian wearing, but it suited my needs just fine.

I found him in the kitchen. "Morning," I said nonchalantly, as I strolled in.

"Good morning." He did a double take. "Where on earth did you find that?"

I shrugged. "In your cupboard somewhere."

"Was the robe not to your tastes?"

"Oh it was fine. I just figured if you were going to hold my clothes hostage I'd do the same to you."

He laughed loudly. "Fair enough. Although I have to say, if commandeering your clothes causes you to dress like this every day, I'm not sure I'll be giving them back any time soon. Are you naked under there?"

I grazed my teeth over my bottom lip and tried to look innocent. "Maybe."

He made an appreciative noise. "Well I have to say, you look fucking sexy wearing my clothes."

"So it is yours?" I asked, grinning widely.

He sighed. "Regrettably, yes. Let's just say I was going through a phase."

I laughed. It was impossible to picture Sebastian looking anything other than perfectly dapper — even now, naked, save for a pair of loose fitting slacks, he looked stunning — but it was nice to know he was human too.

My stomach rumbled as my brain finally registered the smell of oil and eggs. Looking around, I realised that breakfast was already well on the way. There was coffee brewing in a rather elaborate drip filter pot, and several fry pans were sizzling on the stove. Sebastian was busy flitting between them, spatula in hand. There was something about the image that made me giggle.

"What's so funny?" he asked.

"Nothing, I just didn't take you for much of a cook."

A look of mock offence crossed his face. "And why would you think that?"

"I don't know. I just assumed you'd have somebody to do it for you."

"Because money means you never do anything for yourself?"

"I didn't say that! It's just an amusing image. The millionaire dom who liked to cook. It's like a bad erotic book title."

He grinned. "Even us steely sadists have to eat."

"Well it smells great." I slipped closer to survey what was on offer. "Mmm, Chorizo for breakfast? You're living dangerously."

"I do everything dangerously, Sophia," he deadpanned. We both laughed.

"You know, I honestly can't remember the last time a guy cooked me breakfast," I said, taking a seat as he slid a plate in front of me. "I have to say, I kind of like it so far."

He joined me at the bar. "Sounds to me like you've been dating the wrong guys."

"You can say that again." As much as I willed it to stay put, the smile fell from my face. I hated that two years later, Connor still had the power to hurt me, but he did. Just thinking about him made my stomach knot with shame.

Sebastian gazed at me for several seconds, his expression mirroring my own. "He must been one hell of a bastard."

I nodded. "He wasn't exactly boyfriend of the year."

"I'm sorry, I didn't mean to bring him up."

I sighed. As much as it hurt to discuss, I still felt a little like I owed Sebastian an explanation for my past behaviour.

"It's fine. I should be able to talk about this stuff by now."

He hesitated, but took the hint. "What happened between you two exactly?"

"Nothing worth talking about. He was rich and charming, I was young and naive. It was a match made in heaven... for him at least."

"Were you together long?"

"A few years. Long enough to make me feel like an idiot for ever trusting him." It came out more bitter than I'd intended.

"Hey," he said, reaching out to stroke my arm, "everybody's allowed a mistake, here or there. God knows I've got my share."

"There's a difference between a mistake and outright stupidity. All the signs were there — unexplained nights away from home, mysterious texts — but he always had an excuse ready, and I ate them up. Looking back on it now it seems so fucking obvious."

"People don't behave rationally when they're in love. You can't hold that against yourself. Besides, from where I'm sitting, you're not the one that really fucked up."

"Oh?"

He smiled. "You're a strong, beautiful, amazing woman, Sophia. He may have had you for a year or two, but he gave you up. One day, someone is going to have you forever, and then they're going to be the ones making *him* look stupid."

I stared at him for several seconds, a rush of some foreign emotion blazing in my belly. Talking about Connor always left me feeling angry and embarrassed, but somehow Sebastian had washed all that away with just a few lovely words.

"Well, it's hard to argue with that," I said.

"Then don't."

We moved on to lighter topics. Sebastian had several less

than flattering stories about Thomas. I think he was just trying to get revenge for 'Locky'. The whole experience was a bit of a revelation. Every time I was with him, he revealed a new side to himself, and I had to admit, lazy Tuesday morning Sebastian was quickly becoming my favourite. As fantastic as the sex was, it was nice just sitting around and chatting with him too. Away from prying eyes he seemed more relaxed; the professional superman persona was stashed away in the wardrobe alongside his racks of designer suits. Here he was just Sebastian, a man who wore old clothes and cooked scrambled eggs and delivered sweet words over coffee. What's more, he seemed at ease doing those things with me.

In spite of what Thomas had said and the initial discussions between Sebastian and I, it was hard not to feel like things were changing. Our last two nights together had been anything but casual, and it seemed impossible he didn't feel it too. The word 'forever' lingered in my mind. I didn't know how to take that comment. Was there more to it than simple comfort? Part of me wanted to think so.

After breakfast, we found our way back to the bedroom. He told me to leave his shirt on while he fucked me, pinning my arms behind my back and whispering dirty things about how hot I looked in his clothes. There were no cuffs or paddles or lengths of rope, just the unbreakable strength of his hands and the exquisite pressure of his cock. It was more than enough.

Afterwards, we lay snuggled in bed, flushed and glowing and blissfully satisfied. I desperately didn't want the morning to end, although I knew I couldn't delay much longer.

"Has anyone ever told you you tend to go above and beyond the call of duty?" I asked, dozing against his chest.

He began stroking my shoulder. "In what way?"

"Well, I tasked you with cheering me up, but apparently

you weren't satisfied with that. Right now, I've left cheerful way behind. Seriously, you can't even see that shit anymore. I'd say I'm well into blissful territory. You deserve a commendation, sir."

His hand froze. "I'm glad you're feeling better."

"Next time, I'm totally going to call in sick and see how far we can push this."

There was a pause. "Next time?"

"Next time we do this. I'll tell you; a girl could get used to sleepovers and homemade breakfasts."

The silence that followed should probably have set alarm bells ringing in my head, but I was too content to really notice. All I could think about was how for the first time, it felt like things were really coming together for us.

How wrong I was.

Chapter 10

It turned out that I needn't have worried about being relegated to the bench again. The Wrights case had hit the front page once more after a new batch of victims came forward, so we were ramping up our efforts. For now, it was all hands on deck.

It was fascinating, and a little horrifying, to be a part of. A perfect illustration of the power mega companies can bring to bear when profits are under threat. I was no stranger to the greed of big business, but there was a callousness about their approach that made even me balk. They were like a truck, calmly driving along, ignoring every traffic signal. Most people managed to dive out of their way, but those that didn't weren't even worth a second glance. They were just squashed underneath like bugs. In spite of the pain and hassle a proper trial would involve, part of me hoped they refused to settle. The more I read, the more I wanted Little Bell to crush them in the court room.

Nothing came of the situation with Jennifer, so I figured she'd just been messing with me for her own enjoyment. I felt a little stupid for overreacting. It wasn't a big deal in the grand scheme of things.

I should have been happy that I was finally working on

my dream project, but I couldn't really enjoy it. Something had changed with Sebastian. There was no doubt in my mind anymore that my feelings for him had grown, but ever since our morning together, his seemed to have moved in the opposite direction.

It wasn't that he was ignoring me. He still messaged every day or two, but they were short and monosyllabic and lacked any of the warmth I'd come to expect. In person he was no better. Aloof, almost to the point of being cold, we rarely had a discussion that lasted more than a few minutes. That amazing man from just a few nights ago was nowhere in sight.

I clung on, hoping it was just stress. Over the next two weeks, our encounters took on a fairly predictable rhythm. A spontaneous text message, a frenetic sexual rendezvous, and then a hasty departure. On the surface, it was great. I was working overtime, even by my standards, and it was the sort of comfortable arrangement that fit perfectly around that. The problem was that wasn't the kind of comfort I was looking for anymore. I often found my mind wandering back to that morning chatting over coffee, and to the night before, to the overpowering rightness I'd felt as I drifted off to sleep cocooned in his arms. And the more I thought, the more I longed for that closeness again.

"You could stay, you know," I said to him one night, as he stood up and began to gather his things.

"I really should get home." He even looked different now. There was a permanently harried cast to his eyes that I'd never seen before.

"Is everything okay?" I'd tried several times to pry something out of him, even the tiniest hint of what had gone wrong, but it was useless.

He nodded. "Yeah. I just have a lot to do, that's all." He tried shooting me a reassuring smile, but it didn't quite cut through the hardness on his face.

I didn't understand. Our connection had felt so real and so powerful to me, and I'd been so sure he felt it too. But now I was starting to doubt myself.

Maybe I really had just imagined everything. Maybe I had no idea how to read men at all. My past relationships certainly said as much. But if that was the case, could I keep going the way things were, knowing there was nothing more to it? It felt wrong to throw away something that was so theoretically perfect, but every night that we said goodbye, I felt my heart break just a little more.

Still, I wasn't quite ready to give up just yet. People always said the way to a man's heart was through his stomach, and that was one approach I had yet to try. So when the weekend rolled around, I sent him a text.

Sophia: Hey. Hope they're not working you to the bone over there. I thought maybe you could come around for dinner tonight night if you're free. I'm not much of a chef, but I do make a mean carbonara. Thought I could pay you back for breakfast the other week. Let me know.

He replied a few minutes later.

Sebastian: Not sure I should. But maybe I can swing by later on?

I'd expected it, but I still felt a pang of disappointment.

Sophia: Okay, sure.

But as the day progressed, my frustration grew. I kept turning his message over in my mind. It was the phrasing that

98

bothered me. There was that word *"should"* again. *"Not sure I should."* That wasn't the same as *"Not sure I can."* It could mean that he was too busy or had something else on, but it could also mean that he simply didn't want to. If that was the case, then I was wasting my time. I tried to convince myself to stop overthinking it, but by the time the evening rolled around, I still felt uneasy.

Mostly out of stubbornness, I made a pot of carbonara anyway, and ate a bowl of it while reading on the couch. There wasn't much to do but wait. He hadn't given an exact time.

At about eleven o'clock, there was a knock at the door.

"Sophia," he said by way of greeting.

"Hey." Even with the turmoil I felt, I found myself smiling. It was good to see him. There was something addictive about the way I felt when we were together, some beautiful nexus of hormones and emotions that made everything seem a little brighter, a little more real. I desperately wanted to keep feeling that as often as possible.

Not even waiting until we'd made it inside, he moved in to kiss me, and for a few seconds, my body began to yield to his. But as he pressed me up against the hallway wall, his hand already teasing the curve of my ass, I felt something crack inside me.

"Sebastian... wait..." I said, forcing myself to pull back.

"What? Is something wrong?"

I closed my eyes for a second and cupped my face in my hands. "Just once in a while could we maybe wait more than a few minutes before you start feeling me up?"

His smile slipped. "I'm sorry. I just missed you, that's all. You know what your body does to me."

"It sounds like you missed my body a lot more than the rest of me," I replied, a little more harshly than intended.

He didn't seem to know how to reply to that.

Suddenly feeling uncomfortable in such an intimate position, I ducked under his arm and moved into the lounge room. He followed me in silence.

"I'm not sure I understand," he said, after about twenty seconds.

"Well that makes two of us." I hadn't planned to go on the offensive tonight, but the churning feeling in my stomach couldn't be ignored any longer.

"Did I do something wrong?" he asked.

I laughed bitterly and shook my head. "Nope. You've done basically everything just the way you promised."

"So what's the problem?" I didn't respond. "Is it about dinner?"

I threw up my hands. "Yes... no... I don't know. I thought it would be nice, that's all. Spend a little time together. You've been distant, lately."

"We've seen each other three times this week."

I shot him a pointed look. "Distant and physically present aren't mutually exclusive."

He ran a hand through his hair and began pacing. He always seemed to do that when things didn't go to plan, as though enough steps would simply carry him away from the problem all together. "I don't understand what you want from me, Sophia."

"I want some bloody consistency. Why is it okay for you to cook me breakfast, but I can't make you dinner? Why is it okay for me to stay over at your place, but you won't ever stay here?"

There was a pause. "I don't know. I didn't plan any of that, it just sort of happened."

"So? That's how these things are supposed to go. They

100

progress gradually. What I want to know is, why are you trying so hard to make sure it doesn't 'just happen' again?"

He shifted awkwardly and looked away. "Like I said, I've been extremely busy lately. I just don't have that much time—"

"It's not just about the time! It's everything; the way you act, the way you talk to me. It's like there are two different Sebastians. Some days I get the kind, sweet, intensely passionate man who makes me feel wonderful, and other days it's his evil twin who barely wants to do anything but fuck, and who ignores me for weeks on end. How the hell am I meant to deal with that?"

He pursed his lips. "I'm the same man I always was."

"That's what I'm worried about."

His face was a mask of intensity now. "So what are you saying, Sophia?"

I shook my head slowly. There was no going back now. "You want me to spell it out? Okay, fine. You were right to be worried at the beginning; apparently your 'charms' are just too strong. I'm no longer happy just to write this thing off as a casual fling. Don't get me wrong, the sex is great, but it's more than that to me now. I like being with you, Sebastian, naked or not, and I can't go on doing whatever the hell it is we're doing anymore without admitting that. I thought maybe you felt the same way, but apparently I was wrong."

I must have watched one too many sappy romantic comedies, because I was actually disappointed that my declaration didn't cause him to break into a glorious smile and sweep me up in his arms. Instead, he stared at me with an unreadable expression, his jaw working wordlessly.

That silence was almost crushing. A car horn blared somewhere in the distance, punctuating his lack of response. "Say something for god's sake," I said, after a few seconds.

"I'm thinking," he replied.

White hot rage filled me. "*Thinking*? This isn't a moment for thinking Sebastian. This isn't a game anymore. There are no smooth lines to deliver, no different angles to approach from. If you have to think, then this whole thing is a lost cause!"

He continued to sit, utterly motionless, his expression hard as stone.

It was too much. I shot to my feet, suddenly desperate to be anywhere but in his presence. I couldn't even meet his eyes anymore. I should have known better than to expect something more from him. "I need you to leave," I said. "Consider our 'arrangement' over. I'm sure that will give you plenty to think about."

I began moving towards the staircase, but as I passed him, his hand snaked out and caught my wrist. "Sophia, wait. Look at me." His voice was a dry rasp. Barely human.

Reluctantly I turned. The look on his face was frightening enough to stop me in my tracks. It was like his expression so far had just been a mask, and now the entire thing had just broken right up the middle. His cheeks were pinched and flushed, his mouth drawn tripwire tight, and there was something new in his eyes, something I could only describe as terror. It was so intense that I could practically feel it rippling in the air around me. There was no way I was misinterpreting that. Ending this frightened him as much as it did me.

"It's not just me, is it?" I asked, my voice surprisingly soft.

He gave a tiny shake of his head. "Of course it's not just you."

I sank heavily back into my seat. That admission didn't make me feel as good as I'd expected. It lifted one weight while replacing it with another.

"So what is it, Sebastian?" I asked. "If we both want the

same thing, why run away?"

He drew a deep breath. "It's complicated. I'm complicated."

"*Relationships* are complicated," I replied. "There's no avoiding it. We made a good effort at minimising all that and just sticking to the fun stuff, but I for one can't go on that way anymore. As inconvenient as it might be for both of us, this thing means something to me now, and I want everything that comes with that, including your complications."

He gazed into my eyes, a ghost of a smile touching his lips. "It means something to me, too."

"Then stop pushing me away!"

He hung his head. "I want to. I really do. But you don't know what you're asking. You terrify me, Sophia. I've never felt so consumed by another person before. And every time we see each other, it's like I lose another piece of myself in you. You criticise me for thinking too much, but the truth is, around you I don't think. I just do. I have no control. I'm sorry if I freaked out, but I don't know how to deal with that."

They were the most bittersweet words I'd ever heard. His feelings were as strong as mine, but apparently that was only half the battle.

"Why are you so afraid, Sebastian?"

He studied me for what felt like an eternity. I knew this was the moment that would make or break us. He could throw his armour back on, pull down his mask, and march out the door, and there would be nothing I could do to stop him.

"Have you ever lost someone?" he asked eventually. "Someone important?"

I felt a sinking feeling in my stomach. "Two grandparents, although I was too young to remember one very well."

He nodded. "I've lost more than my fair share, but one

cut a little closer to the bone than the rest."

I knew instantly who he was talking about. "The girl in your phone background?"

He swallowed loudly, then nodded.

I thought about her every now and again. That night outside my house was one of the rare moments I'd seen cracks in Sebastian's impeccable facade. They were the same cracks I could see now, only this time, they were a hundred times worse. What the hell had I just started?

"What happened?" I asked, as gently as I could.

His lips compressed and he gazed down at the table. "Some men broke into her house," he said, his voice completely hollow. "The police said they were probably high, looking for money or something to sell." He gave a sad little laugh. "She was always a fighter. Never backed down from anything. That's one of the things I loved about her." He paused again. "There was a struggle. They beat her senseless. She died before the ambulance even arrived."

My hand flew up to my mouth. "Oh god." I reached out to take his fingers in mine. "I'm so sorry, Sebastian. I didn't mean to make you dredge that up."

"It's okay," he replied, although his expression said otherwise. He looked close to tears. It was jarring seeing him like that. He was always so strong, so in control.

"It was serious?" I asked tentatively.

He smiled the most gut-wrenching smile I'd ever seen. "You could say that. We were engaged."

"Oh god," I said again. I had no idea what to say. It was the kind of grief I knew no words would soothe. Even though I'd wanted to know, part of me felt awful for putting him through this. It kind of put my commitment issues into perspective. All I'd done was make a few terribly naive choices; he'd lost the person he loved most in the world. I had no idea how I'd recover from something like that. I suspected I wouldn't.

He closed his eyes and drew several long breaths. "I nearly told you that night outside your house, you know. Nobody besides my closest friends know about Liv, but even then, part of me felt compelled to explain it to you." He brought his eyes up to meet mine, seizing my free hand in his. "There are lots of things I want to share with you, but sharing isn't easy for me. You deserve someone who can give you everything, and I'm afraid if we go any further, I'm going to disappoint you."

For the short period I'd known him, Sebastian had always been a mystery to me. It was like watching a magician perform. I knew there was a trick there somewhere, but I was too dazzled to spot it. But in that moment, I felt like I finally understood him just a little. Behind all those walls, behind that radiant charm and those perfect features, lay a scared and lonely man. I hated seeing him like that, but at the same time, his candour filled me with hope. I knew how much of a gift he'd given me.

"One step at a time, hey?" I said. "I don't need to know all of your deepest, darkest secrets right away. All I need to know is that this is real, because if we go any further and I find out that it's not, I think it will break me."

He studied me for several seconds, a small smile managing to puncture through his otherwise grim expression. "This is the realest thing I know, Sophia."

And then before I could even finish processing what he'd said, he was kissing me. This time I didn't try to stop him. I couldn't. I was certain if anything were going to break that moment, the very planet would have to collapse off its axis. In that kiss, I saw a vision of everything I'd ever wanted. And it was wonderful.

Chapter 11

It's amazing the difference one night can make. Weeks' worth of tension and uncertainty, all dissipated with a single conversation. I woke with my body pressed against his, feeling more content than I had in a long time. The smile on his face when he opened his eyes said that he felt the same.

After a leisurely love making session that involved several creative uses for a dressing gown tie, we headed for the kitchen to squeeze in a quick breakfast before work. Now that we'd acknowledged our feelings, it was more difficult than ever to say goodbye. I really just wanted to spend the whole day together, but that was the peril of a relationship between two dedicated professionals. Time was a limited commodity.

Thankfully we had phones. I used to mock those couples who seemed to require constant contact. I had a friend at university who spent every day glued to her phone, eagerly waiting for the next inevitable text from her boyfriend. It wasn't like they were long distance or anything. She'd see him every night after class. I never understood why she couldn't just wait a few hours to say what she had to say. But now I finally got it. There was something comforting about those little connections. It wasn't so much the words themselves as what they symbolised; that someone out there was thinking of you. And

Sebastian and I made sure to let each other know that as often as possible.

Two days later, I woke up to find a message from him.

Sebastian: You're coming out with me tonight.

I couldn't help but smile. No request. Just an order.

Sophia: And what if I have plans?

Sebastian: I won't be stood up for a stack of subpoenas and a glass of red.

Sophia: Haha. You know me too well. Fine. Where should I meet you?

Sebastian: I'll come to you. I want it to be a surprise. Be home and ready by 6.30. And wear comfortable shoes.

Of course. Why tell me what we were doing when he could just keep it shrouded in mystery instead? I had to hand it to him, he knew how to keep a girl guessing. The comfortable shoes tidbit was interesting. It seemed to imply that we'd be walking somewhere, but I'd long since learned that his hints could rarely be taken at face value.

As usual, my excitement made the day go by at a crawl. This would be our first full night together with everything laid out on the table. For the first time, I could be completely unashamed of the way he made me feel. That was a truly glorious prospect.

When five thirty rolled around, there was still a mountain of work needing to be done. The Wrights case had everyone with their noses to the grindstone. In times past, I'd blown off dates under such circumstances, but the thought didn't even enter my head tonight. I tidied up what I could, sent a few quick apologetic emails, and headed home. Little Bell had been my top priority for six long years; it could spare me the odd night here and there.

Sebastian was perfectly on time as usual. As I stepped out of the front door, he cast his eyes over me and made a little throaty sound. "You're a sight for sore eyes."

I grinned. "We saw each other two days ago."

"And every minute of those was agony," he replied with a dramatic flourish. He did a double take when he spotted my shoes. "The princess is wearing her slippers out again I see."

I'd wondered if he'd notice they were the same pair from that first night. In my experience, men didn't pay much attention to shoes, but Sebastian didn't seem to miss anything. "Well, after the prince so graciously returned them to her, she figured she should make good use of them. Besides, they're the most comfortable shoes she owns."

"Fair enough."

I curled my hands through his hair and pulled his mouth towards mine. God, I'd missed him. In that moment, I was certain I would have been quite happy just standing on my front step with our lips locked together for the rest of the night.

As if reading my thoughts, he pulled away. "Easy now. Let's not get ahead of ourselves. There will be plenty of time for that."

I made a show of pouting, but let him lead me to the car anyway.

The trip was longer than I'd expected. Rather than dropping us somewhere in the city, Joe continued to drive out over the Harbour Bridge.

"Where are you taking me?" I asked, more than a little

curious by now.

But he merely smiled. "If I told you, it wouldn't be a surprise."

Once we crossed the Spit Bridge, I had a better idea, and my suspicions were proven right when we pulled up outside the Manly boardwalk. Manly is one of the suburbs that sprawls along the north side of Sydney Harbour. It's a lovely area; a dynamic mix of beach culture and nightlife. I'd had several messy nights there in my youth, although not for a few years. Old age had made me cynical and territorial, and I tended to stick closer to home now.

"Ah, so another waterfront meal is it?" I asked, feigning disinterest.

He gazed down at me in amusement. "Would it be a problem if it was?"

"Oh, I guess not," I said, trying to hide my smile. "You may want to consider some new material, that's all."

"You underestimate me, Sophia. I've got a few more tricks up my sleeve yet."

Linking arms with me, he led me along the pier. I'd expected him to take me into one of the softly lit, glass panelled restaurants that looked out over the bay, but instead he guided me into the back streets. After just a few minutes of walking, we were essentially in suburbia. I kept my mouth shut now, content to just wait and see.

Eventually we ducked into an alley which appeared to be lined with houses. Sebastian stopped and exchanged a few words with a man who was standing outside a fairly unremarkable doorway. After a few moments, we were led inside and down a narrow staircase. The whole thing had a clandestine feel to it, much like that first night we met, and much like that night, I was not disappointed by what I found.

"Wow," I said, as we reached the bottom. "This is awesome."

I had been half right. It was a restaurant, but it was one of the liveliest restaurants I'd ever seen. The room was packed full of people, all sitting at long tables laughing and chatting and passing around colourful plates laden with food. The air was heavy with a million fragrances, garlic and paprika and the sweet bite of fresh chili. The whole place had an amazing vibe, like everyone had a tacit agreement to shed their troubles for one night and just enjoy themselves. I would have been surprised to spot a single unsmiling face.

"Welcome to Mi Casa," Sebastian said.

"My house?" I asked, vaguely conjuring the translation from some long forgotten primary school Spanish class.

He nodded.

"A bit of a strange name for a restaurant."

His smile widened. "It's not just a restaurant. Come on, they're holding a table for us." Taking my hand, he led me up to the front counter. The man there recognised him instantly, and after a few emphatic words, he guided us towards the back of the room.

"This is my favourite place in the whole of Sydney for a night out," Sebastian said, once we were seated. "I don't get to come here very often anymore, but every time I do, I enjoy myself."

"I can see why," I said.

Without us even having ordered, a waiter appeared at our table bearing two glasses and a tall jug of sangria.

"Standard issue," said Sebastian, with a wink. I wasn't complaining. It was delicious, sweet and rich, but with a hint of spice.

After studying the rather intimidating menu, I gave Sebastian leave to just order for the both of us. There were so many dishes that I had no idea where to start.

It was certainly a far cry from the last restaurant he'd taken me to. Quay had been quiet and sophisticated; the epitome of fine dining. This felt more like a well-kept family secret. From the plastic table cloths to the gregarious patrons, to the giant, warming plates of food, it was the kind of place that instantly made you feel at home. At one point, while Sebastian was ordering, he actually had to start yelling because a group behind us spontaneously broke into song.

"Sorry," he said to me, when the waiter had gone. "This place can get a little rowdy."

"Don't apologise. I love it. Who doesn't want a little show with their meal?"

"Well, the meal will be even better than the show. The food here is out of this world. One of the only places that does paella as good as back home."

"I'm looking forward to it." I took a sip of wine. "So you're originally from Spain then? I have to admit, that accent has always confused me."

He nodded. "I get that a lot. I was born there, and my father was Spanish, but my mother was Australian. Growing up, I didn't really watch television or anything, so with just the two of them teaching me to speak, I kind of wound up with a mix of both accents."

"Spanish and Australian, hey? Well, I must say, that's one hell of a hot combination." I thought back to my discussion with Thomas. I longed to know more about Sebastian's past, but I didn't want to push him. He'd already opened up about Liv, I figured the rest would follow when he was ready.

Instead, we played catch up. Finally free to get to know one another, we covered every topic usually reserved for first and second dates; movies, books, music, TV shows. Neither of us had much time for that stuff anymore, but we fit it in where we could. It turned out he was a big horror movie fan, and he loved Jack Reacher books as much as I did.

"He's the kind of practical hero I can get behind," he said.

These were just tiny pieces, almost inconsequential when taken alone, but each one added just a little bit more to the jigsaw puzzle of him that I was slowly assembling in my head.

The food was as good as he'd promised. He'd ordered far too much — enough for a family of five or six — but he waved away my complaints, insisting that I try everything.

"Are you having a good time?" he asked, when we'd about eaten our fill.

"I'm having an amazing time. Although I'm still a little confused as to why I needed comfortable shoes. Are we going to run off our meal later on?"

He smiled like a man who had a secret he was bursting to share. "You'll see soon enough."

About ten minutes later, there was a commotion in the centre of the room. Looking over, I frowned as I spotted the bulk of the floor staff beginning to gather up tables and chairs and stack them to one side. It seemed a little early to be cleaning up, although nobody else appeared to mind. Most of the diners had vacated their seats and were standing to one side watching.

"Kicking us out already?" I asked.

Sebastian laughed. "Hardly. Watch."

The waiters worked with a well-oiled precision, and in a few minutes, all but our corner of the floor was devoid of furniture. I'd had a few drinks by that point, so it still hadn't quite clicked, but a few moments later, the music that had been meandering in the background suddenly grew louder, and the tune went from sedate to bombastic.

"Oh, no way," I said, watching in wonder as the crowd began to drift towards the centre of the room once more, their bodies now weaving in time with the rhythm. The energy in the room instantly spiked through the roof.

"Like I said, not just a restaurant," he replied.

"Apparently not." At that moment, the last piece of the puzzle fell into place. "Oh shit. Are you expecting us to dance?" If I'd been going out with anyone else, that thought might have occurred to me earlier, but Sebastian wasn't the sort of guy I ever pictured going out dancing. The freedom of it seemed so at odds with his iron sense of self-control. I figured it would just make him uncomfortable.

"You look surprised," he said, hopping to his feet.

"I just thought you were more of a scotch and poker kind of guy."

"Can't I be both?"

I shook my head slowly in disbelief. "Just when I think I'm starting to get you pegged down just a little..."

He laughed. "There's a lot about me you don't know, Sophia."

"Does all of it have the capacity to embarrass me as much as this?"

"Oh come on, don't tell me you've never gone out dancing with your friends after a few too many."

"Of course I have," I replied, "but replace 'a few' with 'a lot'. I'm certainly not that drunk yet. Besides, that was always at a club. If you can stumble in a circle with your arms over your head, you fit right in in those places. This is different. This looks like an audition for So You Think You Can Dance."

I wasn't exaggerating. I didn't have the knowledge or vocabulary to describe everything that was going on in front of me, but it felt like everyone in the room had at least some kind of dance training. Couples writhed together in perfect unison, their movements wild, yet graceful and assured. No two routines were quite the same. Some pairs clung to one another like lovers on a bed, swaying and rocking in a permanent embrace. Others moved with more swagger, an ever shifting whirlwind of bare legs and muscular arms. There was something incredibly sensual about it all. I felt almost voyeuristic just sitting on the sidelines watching.

"You're overthinking it Sophia. Remember what you said to me the other night? 'If you have to think then this whole thing is a lost cause.'" He pulled me to my feet. "You probably don't pay attention to the way you move, but I certainly do, and that body is made to dance."

I looked on helplessly as waiters swept in to clear our table away too. "I thought dancers were meant to be tall and thin."

He smiled a wicked smile and ran a hand gently down my hip. "Ballet dancers perhaps, but that's not really what I have in mind." He nodded once more towards the throng. "Come on, all you have to do is follow my lead."

Maybe it was the pull of the music, or the seductive energy of the dancers, I'm not sure, but I found myself nodding. He led me into the fray.

Instantly, I felt the adrenaline of the crowd wash over me. It was a tangible thing that filled the air, seeping through my skin and setting my body thrumming. The speakers were blasting out a driving rhythm, something modern, but with a distinctly Latin bent, and Sebastian was quick to find his stride. I don't know how I'd ever thought he'd look awkward. One glance at that lithe body and anyone could see how at home he was on the dance floor. His innate sexuality translated savagely well to such expression. Every gesture, every subtle shift of his hips, made him look even more alluring.

Pressing one hand to the small of my back and seizing my fingers with the other, he began to lead me across the room, his feet a rhythmic blur, his body undulating like a flag in the breeze. I didn't want to make him look like a fool, so I tried my best to match him, but my muscles felt stiff in his hands. The show going on around us was elaborate, chaotic, beautiful, and I had no idea how I could possibly match it. I felt impossibly out of my depth.

"You're still thinking," said Sebastian, sensing my discomfort. "Stop focusing so hard. This is meant to be fun, not a competition. The room doesn't exist. They don't exist. It's just you, me, and the music."

I liked that idea. Closing my eyes, I leaned in against him and tried to relax. It was easier with everything out of sight. All I had to go by was the churning beat of the speakers and the touch of Sebastian's hands. Gradually, I let my muscles go soft, trusting that he would guide me. The throbbing bass was like a beacon, and I let my body follow as it desired.

"Much better," Sebastian said.

I had no name for what we were doing. Maybe I still looked stupid, I didn't know, but I no longer cared either way. It just felt right. I loved the sensation of being pressed up against him, letting him steer my limbs as though they were an extension of his own. In that moment, we were one entity moving in perfect harmony. It felt more than a little like when we made love — his hands manipulating me as my body bent to his, yielding to his control — and it was no less exciting for us being fully clothed.

But beyond the physical element, there was something deeper. I knew it was a side of him that he rarely shared, which made it all the more special that he was doing so with me. One by one, his walls were tumbling down.

As the first song ended, the music changed. The new tune was slower, more sultry, and Sebastian was quick to adapt. A delicate twist of his wrist and I was spinning away, then suddenly snapping backwards to rest against him once more, this time with my back against his chest. With torturous softness, his hands began to trace their way across my sides and down my thighs, flirting with the hem of my dress. Such intimacy in a public place should have made me balk, but the sensuality in the air was infectious. I was utterly lost in the moment. I could feel his breath hot on my skin as his lips teased the air just above my neck, tantalising but never touching. With every vacillation of our hips my ass grazed against his pants, letting me know that I wasn't the only one finding this to be a powerfully erotic experience.

Other couples were throwing propriety to the wind too. Several men swept passed us with open shirts, their chests glistening with sweat, their partners slicing the air with their skirts like fans. One woman had shed her top all together and was twisting from side to side in just her bra like a belly dancer. All around the room, people were laughing and clapping and cheering in time with the beat. I'd never been part of such an unrestrained expression of joy before.

"You look stunning," Sebastian breathed into my ear.

"Do I now?" I replied.

"You do. Although it might have something to do with the fact that everything you're doing right now, I'm imaging you doing it naked."

I laughed. "Is that so? Well then, I probably shouldn't do this." Slipping free of his grip, I turned once more and began to glide around him in a slow circle, swaying my hips provocatively and dragging my hands slowly up and down my body.

A low, masculine sound escaped his throat. "God, I can only restrain myself so much, Sophia."

I grinned, but didn't stop. It was thrilling putting on that kind of show for him in the middle of a crowded room. I could see the outline of his excitement pressing urgently against his pants. The truth was, with all the electricity that was coursing through my veins, I wasn't sure I wanted him to restrain himself. I'd had the elaborate foreplay, now I wanted what that promised.

He didn't disappoint. At the end of my second orbit, he seized me once more and pulled me in for a kiss. The intensity in that gesture was almost overpowering, and for a few moments, I lost all sense of where we were or what we were doing. All that existed was the two of us, our tongues dancing together like our bodies just had.

When he finally backed away, snatched my hand, and began leading me from the dance floor, I didn't say a word. It was a ludicrous thing to be considering with a roomful of people around us, but the longing I felt dwarfed all sense of logic.

Somehow, he found a little privacy; a small function room hidden behind a curtain at the back of the room. It didn't provide much protection — there were no locks, nor even a real door — but I don't think there was an obstacle in the world that would have stopped us at that moment. Taking a second to unzip his fly and pull himself free, he looped his hands under my thighs and lifted me up, bracing me against the wall. I wrapped my legs around him, and then with a flick of his wrist, he nudged my panties aside and rammed his shaft inside me.

Heat instantly tore through me.

"You see how you make me lose control Sophia?" he rasped, his face contorted in pleasure. "I'm addicted to you. It's not enough. It's never enough." Every statement was punctuated by a powerful pivot of his hips.

I moaned and buried my face against his shoulder, content to let him take from me as much as he wanted. Every nerve in my body already felt like it was vibrating, but with each forceful stroke Sebastian strummed my arousal just a little more. My legs tightened around his hips like a vice, pushing him deeper still, spurring him on.

"Harder." My voice sounded strained.

"Ask properly," he purred, nibbling my earlobe.

"Fuck me harder, Sebastian. Please."

For a moment he slowed. Then, angling my legs slightly, he slammed back into me. I cried out, nearly biting down on his flesh in the process. His plunges became punishing, almost to the point of pain, but my body swallowed each one as hungrily as a breath of air. I loved that desire, that raw, unrestrained need. Every stroke was a reiteration of a promise. *"You are mine, every inch of you."*

My back arched, my hips trying to add their own motion to the equation, but there was no space for me to move, nowhere for me to go. I was pinned helplessly against the wall, being fucked less than twenty feet from a cheering, surging crowd. And it felt amazing.

I could still hear that trembling beat pumping in the next room. The bass of it echoed in my chest. It made our lovemaking feel like just an extension of the dance, our rhythm shifting and slowing in time with the music. It was beautiful; the perfect culmination of the perfect night.

Nudging my head backwards, Sebastian engulfed my mouth with his, the softness of his tongue contrasting deliciously with the firmness of his cock. My hands ran wild across the hard expanse of his back, revelling in the vibration of his muscles as he drove himself into me.

I felt a pressure building in my core, signalling that my body couldn't hold out much longer.

"I'm close," I said breathlessly.

"Then look at me." I brought my forehead up to meet his, placing our eyes just inches apart. "Don't close your eyes.

Don't even blink. I want you to watch me as I make you come, Sophia, every moment of it."

And with a powerful rocking motion, he pushed me over the edge. The rawness, the affection, the risk of getting caught, it was an intensely powerful combination. I clawed at his skin, my whole body quivering with the ecstasy of my release. I'm fairly sure I screamed, but with the noise in the next room, nobody seemed to notice.

His turn came soon after. With several final bestial pumps his fingers dug deep into my legs, his body stiffening to iron as he burst inside me.

As his pleasure faded, he shook his head slowly. "You know, one of these days you're going to get us into trouble, Sophia."

"Me?" I asked, trying to look innocent. It was difficult. He still held me pinned in the air, his semi-erect penis still buried inside me. "I believe you were the one that dragged me in here and ravished me without so much as asking."

He raised an eyebrow. "I do seem to remember warning you of the consequences of your actions. And if you're going to pretend you didn't enjoy yourself, I may be forced to prove you wrong." His mouth dipped down to my neck. "I bet I could make you come again right here against this wall. I bet I could make you scream so loud the entire room out there would hear."

I closed my eyes for a moment, enjoying the soft teasing of his lips. "As wonderful as that sounds, I'm not sure I'm quite ready for a live audience."

"That's okay, neither am I. Now that I've got you, all of this," he nodded towards my body, "is mine and mine alone. I don't want to share even the sight of you."

"Well, if this evening is any indication of the way you take care of your possessions, then I believe that arrangement will work just fine."

After cleaning up and doing our best to make ourselves presentable, we slipped back out into the crowd. Nobody paid us any mind. The room still bore a frenetic energy, and part of me wanted to rejoin the party, but coming that hard had left me feeling a little weak at the knees, so we headed for the door.

I expected Joe to magically appear the way he always seemed to do, but the street outside was empty.

"I think we've been abandoned," I said.

He laughed. "I wouldn't put it past Joe, but that's not the case right now. I thought we could take a walk before leaving."

My arm broke out in goosebumps as a gust of sea breeze swept through the alley. Despite the time of year, the night was unseasonably cold. "I don't know, I'm kind of chilly. Maybe another night?"

"Come on, I want to show you something. It's not far." Removing his jacket, he slipped it over my shoulders. "Better?" he asked.

I smiled. "Ever the gentleman." It certainly was warmer, although I didn't know how he wasn't freezing now. On the plus side, that left him in just a shirt, which showed off the hard curves of his chest considerably better. "Fine, let's go." He wrapped his arm around my shoulder and began to lead me towards the main street. "But I have to say," I continued, "I'm a little uncomfortable with all this romance. Late night walks along the water might send the wrong message. We have boundaries, remember?"

He laughed loudly. "After seeing you shake it like that in there, there's no more boundaries, Sophia. You've officially ruined me for anyone else." He gave my ass a playful slap to illustrate the point.

"Oh, so that's what I have to do to earn a spanking is it?"

I asked, shaking my hips a little.

"Aww, feeling neglected are you?"

I grinned. "Just curious, really. It's been a while since you brought out the heavy artillery in the bedroom. It's enough to make a girl think you've gone soft."

He returned my smile. "I believe I showed you exactly how hard I can be just a few minutes ago."

That made me laugh. "That you did."

"But seriously," he continued, "not every dominant is the same. I have to be in control in the bedroom, that will never change, but we're not all leather wearing, paddle wielding machines. Don't get me wrong, I love a little kink when the mood is right, but truth be told, I think I often used that really hardcore persona as a kind of shield. It was always much easier to keep distance between my partners and I when I was playing a role. But with you, I just want to get as close as possible."

It was still novel hearing him express his feelings for me so openly. It made me tingle all the way down to my toes. "So no more tie up then?" I asked cheekily.

He slipped in behind me and pinned my arms to my side, stopping me in my tracks. "Oh I wouldn't say that." I closed my eyes as I felt him brush his lips gently against my ear before nipping softly at my neck. "There are still plenty of things I want to do to that body of yours. I'm just waiting for the right moment."

"Then I guess I'll just have to be patient," I replied, my voice suddenly breathy.

"Exactly."

We walked in silence for a while. I'd been expecting him to lead me to the beach, but instead he veered off down another side street. My confusion mounted when he turned again, this time off the road all together, onto a narrow dirt path that wove between two houses. Canopied and devoid of

121

street lights, I could barely see more than three feet ahead.

I paused at the opening. "You said you liked horror movies, well this is exactly how most of them start."

He smiled. "Trust me."

We walked for about a hundred feet, the incline growing steeper with every step, until eventually we broke through the other side.

"Wow," I said for the second time that night. The view in front of me was nothing short of spectacular. The hidden track had opened out onto a wide expanse of headland that looked out over Manly Cove. We could see everything; the moonlit shoreline, the forest of yacht masts in the bay, even the electric outline of the city in the distance.

"How did you even find this place?" I asked.

"Luck." He looked sheepish. "Or perhaps stupidity. I'd spent a night at Mi Casa with some friends and we indulged a little too much. I went for a walk, got turned around finding my way back, and somehow wound up here." He gazed out over the churning waves. "I'm kind of glad I did though. I love this view."

"It's beautiful," I agreed.

He led me over to an open space a few feet from the lip of the cliff and we sat down. Leaning in, I laid my head on his shoulder and snuggled close. Although the breeze was even more intense up here, with my body pressed against his, I no longer felt cold.

He nodded towards the docks where several sleek white boats were slowly swallowing and disgorging passengers. "The thing I like most is the ferries. I've always loved ships, even since I was a kid. There's something about the beginning of a journey that fills me with hope."

I couldn't help myself. "You know they're just going to the city, right? Half of them are probably going to wind up throwing up in a gutter in a few hours."

He laughed. "Come on, where's your sense of wonder?" His expression shifted from amusement to something more reflective. "The truth is, I actually got away on a ship."

I hesitated. I could tell straight away that we were venturing into darker territory. It had been such an amazing night, and part of me didn't want to do anything to ruin that perfect vibe, but he'd brought me up here for a reason. I'd said I wanted more openness. I couldn't deny him now. "Got away?"

He licked his lips. "Like I said earlier, I didn't have the easiest time growing up. The place I lived... well, it wasn't exactly fit for kids. Or anyone, for that matter. There were no trains, no buses, not even any real roads. But there was the sea. I used to sit on a point a lot like this and stare at the boats that pulled in and out of the docks on the other side of the bay. I always loved the thought that they were going away. I didn't even care where. Just, away. Eventually, when I was old enough and strong enough, I swam out and stowed away on one and never looked back."

I spent a few seconds processing this. It was a lot to take in. "I thought you said you were from Spain."

He gave a sad little smile. "A lot of people don't realise how much poverty there is in big European countries. My parents and I lived in a little shanty town about an hour outside Barcelona. There's more of them than you'd think. France has hundreds. Portugal too. Entire groups of people who have just slipped through every support network available, until they land in the only place that will take them."

"A shanty-town?" I asked uncertainly.

He nodded, then grimaced. "Our house was made mostly from old plywood doors held together by nails. The roof was a single sheet of corrugated iron. I remember that whenever it rained, it used to make the most awful noise, like a clap of thunder that lasted the entire night."

"Fuck," I said, shaking my head in disbelief. "I can't even imagine living like that. Why didn't your parents do anything? I know if I had a child, I'd do everything in my power to get them away from a place like that."

He nodded. "I used to hate them for that, but I don't anymore. They were good people, I know that now. That sort of life just has a way of sapping your willpower. Everyone there had been defeated so many times they'd almost given up. Besides, when you fall in with those sort of people, even if you do want to leave, it's not as easy as just packing up and hitting the road."

I understood the implication, but the strain in his voice told me not to delve any further. Whatever his parents had or hadn't done, it didn't change the sort of man Sebastian was.

"Well, you got out," I said, smiling and squeezing his hand. It awed me knowing that he'd been through so much and still managed to turn into the magnificent, confident man sitting next to me.

"That I did."

"And you've done rather well for yourself since then. How does one go from shanty town urchin to professional jet-setting millionaire anyway?"

He smiled. "That's a story for another time, I think. Can we just enjoy the view for a while?"

"Okay, sure." A few moments passed. "And Sebastian. Thanks."

He answered by pulling me closer and kissing my hair softly.

I'm not sure how long we sat there. We stayed until long after the last ferry had pulled away from the dock. To tell you the truth, I would have been perfectly content to spend the whole night there, cradled in his arms, his fingers gently stroking my cheek. I'd never felt happier in my entire life.

Chapter 12

Sebastian stayed the night at my place, and the next morning we went out for breakfast. It was a little unprofessional to be late to the office again, especially after ducking out early yesterday, but the truth was that I didn't care. Last night had shown me how perfect our relationship could be, and all I wanted to do was keep feeling that same euphoria for as long as possible.

"What's your schedule like for the next few days?" I asked him, as we were finishing up our coffees.

He grimaced. "Busy, unfortunately. I suspect I'll be eating all my meals at my desk for the foreseeable future. You may have to entertain yourself for a few days."

I felt a pang of disappointment, but I brushed it aside. "Fair enough. We're getting pretty stuck into the Wrights case now anyway, so I won't exactly be bored." I picked up my coffee spoon and drew it in and out of my mouth slowly, dragging my tongue along the underside. "Of course, I may require entertaining once more before you disappear."

He grinned. "You know, it just so happens that I have a block of free time that has just opened up right... now."

Suffice it to say that I was even later to work than I initially planned.

In truth, I wasn't as upset about Sebastian's busyness as I should have been, because he'd given me an idea. His surprises were becoming a regular fixture in our relationship, and I wanted to even the score a little. So I decided that if he was too busy to go out, I'd bring myself to him.

When lunch time rolled around the next day, I picked up a couple of sandwiches from a nearby deli and headed for his building. A little subtle questioning over breakfast had told me that while he did have that office stashed behind the bar, that was only used during functions. He actually spent most of his time at the main Fraiser Capital building, which turned out to be only a ten minute walk from mine.

The building was as impressive as I'd been expecting. A sparkling cylinder of dark glass that shot up into the sky like a raised fist. It was somewhat intimidating being at Sebastian's office. There was nothing overtly strange about it, but the secrecy with which his company approached their work made me feel a little like a soldier venturing behind enemy lines.

I marched up to the front desk, trying my best to look like I belonged.

"Can I help you?" asked the receptionist, smiling a little too widely. She was a pretty young girl, albeit in an overly made up, magazine cover sort of way.

"Yes, I'm here to see Sebastian Lock."

She glanced at the screen in front of her. "Do you have an appointment?"

"Not really. I was hoping to surprise him." I held up the paper bag containing our lunch.

"Oh, I'm sorry, but nobody goes upstairs without an appointment. Company policy."

"I appreciate that, but it's not like I'm a stranger. I'm his girlfriend." It felt a little funny to say that out loud. We'd never used terms like that before. But still, it was true, wasn't it?

The woman behind the counter smiled in that slightly patronising way that people usually reserve for small children. "I'm sorry, but I can't make exceptions. I can call him if you like, maybe get him to come down?"

I exhaled sharply. I had hoped to surprise him in his actual office, but if this was my only option I guess I had no choice. "Okay sure. Thanks."

She tapped a few buttons on the phone and sat patiently, but nothing happened.

"I'm sorry, but he doesn't seem to be in. I could take a message for you if you like."

I closed my eyes and took a deep breath. Perhaps it was a stupid plan. He was a busy man. I should have just organised to see him over the phone like a normal person.

"Sophia?" said a voice behind me.

I turned and came face to face with Sebastian's friend Thomas.

"It is you. I thought so," he said. He managed a small smile, although he didn't look quite as pleased to see me as he had the other night. Apparently Sebastian wasn't the only one under a lot of stress.

I nodded. "Hi, Thomas."

"You here to see Sebastian?"

I felt a glimmer of hope. "Well I was hoping to, but they won't let me up."

He winced. "Yeah, we're not really meant to have guests upstairs. It's a bit draconian I know, but it's the rules."

"But if I went up with you, it'd be okay, right?" I said, flashing him a smile.

He chewed on his lip. "Technically you have to be a client..."

"Please! I was really hoping to surprise him. I only need a

few minutes."

I thought my feminine charms had done the trick, but eventually he shook his head "Sorry. If anyone found out I'd be in a crazy amount of trouble. Hell, Sebastian himself would chew me out. But since you came all the way here, I can go and find him for you if you like. He's in a meeting, but shouldn't be much longer."

I deflated a little, although I don't know why I was surprised. Sebastian had described Thomas as "a company man through and through." Expecting him to break the rules was probably unrealistic.

Still, his offer was better than nothing. "Okay, sure, that'd be great."

He gestured for me to follow. As we walked towards the lift, he glanced down at the bag I held. "A hand delivered lunch? Sebastian's a lucky man."

"It's more out of necessity than romance I fear. We're both so busy we barely get to see one another. I figured fifteen minutes over a sandwich is better than nothing."

"For sure." He was silent for a few seconds. "So things must be going pretty well between you two then."

My strong, independent side hated the goofy smile that bloomed on my face. *Fuck, Sophia, you're practically swooning.* But try as I might, I couldn't get rid of it. "Yeah, I think so."

"That's good. That's good." But something in his tone said he didn't necessarily believe that. I didn't know what to make of it. Did he still worry about Sebastian's ability to commit? I had to admit, I still had the occasional doubts, but our night at Mi Casa had gone a long way to settling those.

After a few more seconds, the lift arrived. "We'll probably be a few minutes," he said, stepping inside. "Feel free to make yourself comfortable." He pointed to a long sofa that rested against the far wall.

"No worries. Thanks, Thomas."

"My pleasure."

I sometimes wonder what would have happened if I'd just done as he asked. It was one of those seemingly inconsequential decisions that turns out to have massive ramifications.

Instead of sitting and waiting, I couldn't resist the urge to have a little wander. It was becoming clear that I may never get the chance to see Sebastian's actual office, but that didn't mean I couldn't check out the building a little. I was still incredibly curious about the sorts of things they did.

The bottom story appeared to be mostly admin staff; young women in blouses and dark pencil skirts bustling back and forward down long corridors. A few of them shot me strange looks, but nobody stopped me, so I figured I wasn't in breach of any major rules.

I didn't intend to wander very far, just enough to get a glimpse of what went on back there, but the place was a maze, and at some point I managed to get turned around. Before I knew it, I found myself standing in a narrow corridor that was devoid of doors or people. It felt like I'd gradually been moving in a loop, so I headed to the end and turned the corner, expecting to be taken back to the main access point.

Instead, I found something that caused my mouth to drop open.

This hallway was shorter, and it had a door. Just one. The access keypad off to one side said that I wasn't going any further in that direction. Not that I needed to. The door itself told me everything I needed to know. There was no signage, nothing to indicate what lay beyond. That is, except for the small golden letter A that was inscribed on the surface.

There was a grinding sensation in my head, the feeling of a host of gears all suddenly clicking into place. I knew now why that symbol had looked so familiar. This wasn't the first door I'd seen it on. I thought back to the night Sebastian and I had met, to the hidden offices I'd inadvertently prowled through. The name tags had thrown me off, but now I remembered; they were all marked the same way.

Something heavy and dark began to claw at my stomach. I'd asked Sebastian outright about the tattoo, and he'd lied. There was clearly a lot more to it than a drunken generic design. All the strange occurrences and eccentricities that he'd talked his way out of raced through my head. The hidden offices, the secret parties, the strange documents, they were all tied to this. They had to be. Each one taken by itself was fairly innocuous, but throw in the dead man on the news, and this one tiny symbol suddenly pulled it all together into something much more sinister.

Who the fuck were these people?

Somehow, I found my way back to the lifts and threw myself down heavily on the sofa. I had no idea what to do. It wasn't fair. Things between Sebastian and I had finally felt like they were making sense. I'd been happy dammit. But now I could feel that slowly bleeding out of me, replaced by an overwhelming sense of fear.

I'd known there were things about his job he had to keep quiet. I'd accepted that. But I'd assumed that meant client names and project details and other random minutia. This was something else entirely. Part of me wanted to just ignore it, to shove it under the rug in the back of my mind and let things continue the way they had been, but I knew that wasn't possible. I had to know what on earth I was dealing with.

A few moments later, the lift doors split open and Thomas and Sebastian strode out. "Well, isn't this a pleasant surprise," Sebastian said, grinning at me, although the smile fell rapidly when he caught sight of my face. "Sophia, what's wrong?"

Thomas seemed to sense my mood had changed. "I've got something to take care of," he said, shooting me a curious look before heading in the direction of the main foyer. I was thankful for the privacy.

I stared at Sebastian for a few seconds, uncertain where to even begin. "Why can't I come upstairs?" I asked eventually.

That seemed to catch him off guard. "Sorry. I know it's a bit strange. It's just company policy."

"So you're not hiding anything up there?"

Something flickered across his face ever so briefly. "What would I be hiding?"

"That's what I'm trying to figure out."

He looked puzzled by that. Slipping onto the seat next to me, he placed one hand gently on my knee. "I don't understand. What's this about?"

I didn't answer directly. "Do you remember what you told me that night outside my house," I said instead, "the night before you went away? 'I promise I'll never lie to you.'"

He nodded slowly. "I remember."

"So why did you?"

There was a pause. "I'm not sure what you mean."

I sighed. I hadn't really expected him to just spill everything of his own accord, but it had been worth a try. "Let me be more direct then. Why is there a door back there," I nodded towards the centre of the building, "that has the same mark on it as the one on your chest?"

His eyes widened. There were a few seconds of stunned silence. "I think you must be mistaken," he said shakily, but even he didn't sound convinced.

I felt a small flash of anger, but I smothered it. I'd already overreacted once with him. I wanted to give him a chance to explain. "Please, at least do me the courtesy of dropping the act now. I'm not stupid, Sebastian. I know what I saw. I saw it that first night we met as well, I just didn't remember until now."

He had a panicked look in his eyes now, his pupils madly darting left and right. "I'm sorry," he said eventually.

"I don't want apologies, Sebastian. I want explanations!"

He ran a hand through his hair and stared down at the floor. "You don't know what you're asking."

"I'm asking for you to be honest with me. That's all. It's pretty clear you're not who you say you are, and between the secret offices, the strange symbols, and the dead foreign dignitaries, this has me confused and to be honest, a little frightened."

His eyes shot up to meet mine, and any lingering doubts I'd had about the connection vanished. "Dead foreign dignitaries?"

I nodded. "I saw a dead man on the news a few weeks ago. A British politician. He had the same tattoo as you, only on his arm. At the time I thought it was just a coincidence, but your reaction basically confirms that it's not."

He gazed at me, his face utterly distraught. It was the look of a man with an impossible choice to make, and it sent a fresh wave of dread rolling through me. After all we'd shared since that night at my house, I'd honestly been expecting us to get past this. It had felt like he finally trusted me, and that it was only a matter of time before the rest of his walls came down too. But now I wasn't so sure. Whatever he was still hiding was apparently bigger than everything else. Was it bigger than what he felt for me?

"This isn't fair, Sophia," he replied eventually. "You knew we had secrets. I never hid that."

This time the surge of anger was bigger. "It isn't fair? Are you kidding me? Look, I understand some jobs deal with sensitive information, and I totally respect that. I'm in the same boat myself with case details. But this is something else entirely. Do you understand how this looks to me? You have a bloody tattoo of some secret company logo on your chest! I can't even begin to imagine what that means."

His fingers clenched and unclenched rapidly, his head shaking back and forward in a steady rhythm, as if he could send everything into rewind through sheer force of will. "Please don't make me do this," he pleaded.

"What choice do I have?" I asked. "How am I meant to be with a man who keeps things like this from me? How can I trust anything you say? I thought I was starting to get to know the man behind the mask, but now I feel like I'm looking at a stranger." Saying it out loud just made the pain worse. I felt heat welling behind my eyes, but I blinked it away. I was *not* going to cry in the middle of his office.

He drew a heavy breath. "Everything you saw was real, Sophia. I'm a lot of things, things that might not be easy to understand, but I'm also the same man I was a few days ago. The man who danced with you and held you and felt so impossibly lucky to wake up next to you. The man who thinks he's falling in love with you."

I recoiled as if struck. Of all the things he could have said to shock me, that was at the top of the list. How could I possibly deal with that?

"Love?" I said, barely able to wrap my mouth around the word. "Seriously? That's how you're going to wriggle out of this one?" I thought I'd been confused before, but that one little word had set off a bomb inside me. My emotions now lay scattered in a thousand tiny pieces.

He looked almost as surprised as me. "I'm not wriggling out of anything. Look, I've kept things from you, that's true, and I'm sorry beyond words for that, but they were only the things I had no choice but to hide. I have never lied to you

134

about the way I feel. *Never.*" There was fire in his voice when he said that, an earnestness that was almost impossible to ignore.

I shook my head. No matter what I said or did, it felt like it would be the wrong decision. I didn't understand this man. This man that could make me feel so treasured one minute, then so alone the next.

"Even if that's true, it's not enough," I replied slowly. *Of course it's enough*, a tiny part of me was screaming, but it was drowned out by the chorus of other voices, all yelling with equal fervour. "I'm not going to pretend like I have any idea what the hell is going on here, but I can't deal with the constant questions anymore, Sebastian. I can't keep finding new secrets behind the curtains."

"I know," he said wearily.

"So can you promise an end to all that?"

There was a long pause, perhaps the longest of my life. It felt like that moment in my house all over again, that agonising wait, the whole relationship teetering on the next words out of his mouth. Only this time, I didn't get the response I'd hoped for.

Eventually, he closed his eyes. "I don't know."

Every muscle in my body tightened. I let out a long breath. "Then there's nothing more to talk about."

I was surprised by how calmly I got to my feet. I expected him to object. He'd proven his tenacity time and time again. But he didn't. He just stared mournfully at the floor and let me walk away.

I caught sight of Thomas on my way out. He was sitting in an armchair a little way around the corner, sorting through some papers, although he gave me a sympathetic nod as I walked passed. Apparently he hadn't gone far after all. So much for privacy.

I made it into the back of a cab before I began to cry. The driver shot me several uncomfortable glances, but my mind didn't have space to focus on him right now. There was too much pain. Too much confusion. I had no idea how I was meant to have reacted to what just happened. The scope of Sebastian's lies still hadn't sunk in. I didn't know what it could possibly all mean.

And then there was that word.

If he'd meant what he said, how could he just let me leave? Love was supposed to be a connection that triumphed over everything else. I tried to convince myself that it was just a ploy, a desperate, last ditch attempt to save what we had. But the pain in his eyes had been so real, the conviction in his voice so strong. It didn't make any sense.

None of it made any sense.

Chapter 13

The next couple of days were rough. I wandered around the office like a zombie. I think that was my body's way of trying to get through work — just shut down completely. It seemed to do the trick. I wouldn't have called myself a model employee, but I made it through most of my tasks with at least some level of competency.

But at night, I couldn't help but turn the situation over and over in my head. The whole thing had left me utterly dumbstruck. Our relationship had gone from perfect to catastrophic in the blink of an eye. What on earth went on behind the doors of Fraiser Capital? I'd run the gamut of possibilities through my head a thousand times. Was Sebastian a secret agent? A gang member? Part of some kind of bizarre corporate fraternity? Each possibility was as ridiculous as the last, but no plausible option seemed to fit.

I wanted to be angry, and a lot of the time I was, but try as I might, I also couldn't push the things he'd said out of my mind. I hated him for making it so difficult. If he'd just kept his mouth shut, I think it would have been easier to let go, to dismiss what we'd had as lust taken too far. But that one word changed everything. It forced me to confront my feelings for him head on.

My history with love was chequered at best. I'd thought I loved Connor, but obviously that hadn't worked out so well. And I'd been going down the same path again with Sebastian — blind adoration for a man who wasn't honest with me. On the other hand, Connor had never made me feel that divine sense of bliss I experienced when Sebastian and I were together. Even now, with everything that had happened, I often found myself longing to just lose myself in his arms. That had to mean something, didn't it?

It made me feel like the biggest fool on the planet, but part of me kept hoping he'd call and explain himself. I didn't know if I could deal with the truth, or if I'd even believe whatever he had to say, but I hated that he didn't try. It was a coward's move to invoke that word and then not fight.

The weekend passed quietly. I was starting to feel a little better. The initial feeling of panic had ebbed away, replace by a kind of grim acceptance. He wasn't going to call, and that was okay. It seemed devastating now, but the world would keep spinning. *One day at a time*, I told myself. *It can only get better from here.*

I was wrong.

On Monday morning, I got a call from Ernest.

"Sophia, could I see you in my office for a moment?"

Ernest wasn't much of a face to face manager. He preferred the buffer offered by phones and email. To be called in to see him was either very good or very bad, but the sinking feeling in my belly told me it was probably the latter.

"Okay, I'll be right over," I said, a small tremor evident in my voice.

As soon as I opened his door and saw Alan sitting calmly at the desk, that fake smile spread across his face like lumpy butter, my fears were confirmed.

"Sophia," he said, "please, sit down."

Ernest looked almost sheepish, like he felt guilty about leading me into an ambush. I tried to muster a little token anger but, truth be told, it didn't make much difference. If Alan himself had called, I would have had to go just the same.

I did as I was told, sliding into one of the guest chairs that faced the two of them. I suddenly felt cold, the kind of chill that seems to seep right into your bones. I was fairly sure I knew what was coming.

"I'm going to get straight to the point, Sophia," Alan said. He'd do most of the talking. Ernest was just here as a courtesy, most likely. "We need to have a talk about your performance recently."

I stayed silent. I figured I may as well make the conversation as difficult as possible for them.

"To be frank, it hasn't been up to par," he continued.

"In what way?" I asked. My voice was strangely quiet, almost dangerous. It seemed to catch him off guard.

"Well look, you must understand, we respect that work/life balance is important—"

"I'm not in the mood for your bloody jargon, Alan," I interrupted. "Just spit it out."

He rocked back a little in his chair, reflexively tugging at his suit jacket. At least I had him off balance. "Well, you've been arriving late, leaving early, taking long lunches, that kind of thing. Like I said, our goal isn't to work you to the bone, but this firm expects a certain level of commitment which at the moment you're not reaching."

In a way he was right. I had been lax lately, but the injustice of it ran like fire through my veins nonetheless. "I bet if you went back and looked at the last few years," I said, "you'd find I've billed more hours overall than any other associate on this floor. Probably more than you yourself."

He bristled. "I don't know about that. In any case, we all

appreciate your dedication to the company. But you can't just rest on your laurels in this business. And the fact remains that your recent work has not be up to standard."

I hated how he kept using the word 'we', like he and Ernest were somehow cohorts in this little game. Ernest couldn't have looked more uncomfortable if he'd tried.

"So what is this? Am I being fired?"

Alan gave a little laugh, one that was as fake as his smile. "Now, let's not be hasty. We know as well as anyone that this job can get overwhelming at times. No, we just feel that your poor attendance, coupled with recent events, mean that—"

"Recent events?" I said, my tone somehow growing colder still.

He hesitated once more, but I didn't need him to fill in the blanks. I'd done so the moment I walked through the door.

"You mean with Jennifer?" I finished.

The dip in his expression confirmed it. I'd underestimated her. That little weasel really did want me gone, and between my recent lapses in attendance and my reaction to her prank, I'd handed her all the ammunition she needed to make it happen.

"She mentioned that you'd ignored some of her instructions, yes."

"Did you actually read what those instructions were?" I hissed.

Something in my voice must have jarred him to his senses, because he sat up straight in his chair, seeming to realise exactly who outranked who. "That's not really relevant," he said, his voice growing stern. "I trust Jennifer to do the right thing. What this comes down to, Sophia, is attitude. It's about showing you're a team player. Work is distributed the way it is for a reason. When people start going off on their own, things begin to break down. Jobs slip through the cracks. Everyone has their role to play. If you can't understand that, then maybe you *don't* belong at Bell and Little."

Ernest still hadn't said a word.

"And what do you think about all this, Ernest?" I said. I didn't really expect him to leap to my defence, but it was worth a shot.

He shifted in his chair. "I think that this isn't you, Sophia." He looked almost sad when he said it.

Alan cleared his throat. "What I was trying to say before is, we think maybe you should take a little time off. You've got a significant amount of leave built up. Why not use it to get your head right? There's no shame in saying you need a little R and R."

It was phrased as a suggestion, but that was just an illusion. I was being exiled. It might not have sounded like a big deal — a little holiday, then back to the grind — but I knew better. It was really a dismissal in disguise. That's how Alan liked to operate; ease someone out of the office quietly, and then let the axe fall. Much less messy that way. I could see it in Ernest's eyes. He knew I wasn't coming back.

Strangely, I wasn't really upset. I figured maybe that would come later. Instead, the numbness coating my insides just seemed to thicken. Truth be told, I'd expected it — or something similar — the moment I walked through the door.

I stood up. There was no point in arguing. "Okay."

"Okay?" Alan asked.

"Okay, I'll take some time."

And without another word I turned and left.

I snatched my bag from my office and then made straight for the lift. I desperately wanted to avoid talking to anyone. The wafer thin barricade was holding my emotions in check was ready to burst at any moment.

But of course, she couldn't resist her chance at a parting shot.

Leaning against an office doorway near the lifts, was Jennifer. She was chatting idly with the person inside, but there was no doubting her true purpose. She caught sight of me from across the room as I approached. There were no words, no taunts or mockery, just the smallest upturn of her lips and a victorious flash in her eyes. She'd won and she knew it.

I fled. I didn't even bother waiting for the lift, I just bolted down the fire escape as fast as I could. Everything was unravelling before my eyes.

I had to get away from that place.

Chapter 14

I'm not certain exactly how I got home. I think I took a taxi, although I can't be sure. All I remember was being overcome by a great wave of tiredness. The moment I walked through the door, I threw myself into bed, pulled the covers over my head, and slept.

When I woke it was dark. The power was out. There was no storm that I could hear, just a horrendous wind that was screeching up and down the narrow alleys that surround my house.

Glancing at my phone, I discovered it was ten o'clock. I also saw that I had several missed calls from Elle. No doubt word had gotten around. Gossip spread faster than the plague in our office. She was probably worried, but I couldn't deal with talking to her yet.

I really wished I could just go back to sleep. The enormity of everything that had happened was absolutely staggering. I didn't know how to begin dealing with it all. It made the prospect of simple unconsciousness incredibly appealing. But I could tell I wouldn't drift back off again.

Not knowing what else to do, I lit some candles and went to the kitchen to pour a bowl of cereal. I wasn't particularly hungry, but I figured I probably needed to eat. It tasted like shredded cardboard, but I barely noticed.

Halfway through my meal, everything finally caught up with me. One minute I was staring blankly down at my food, the next I was bawling my eyes out. I'd never felt so utterly lost before. My life had always felt like it had been on rails, with the next stop visible just a little way up the track. School, a law degree, internships, a job; everything had unfolded as planned. But now suddenly, the track had collapsed underneath me, leaving me wobbling at the edge of a precipice. I had no idea where to go from here.

It was soul destroying to watch six years of hard work crumble to dust before my eyes. The prospect of starting again from scratch was impossibly daunting. I lay my arms on the breakfast bar and buried my head between them, sobbing until I felt like my eyes were just empty husks.

The worst part was, I had no way to distract myself. I was going to wake up tomorrow with nothing to do. And the day after that. And the day after that. That was a terrifying prospect. I thrived on hard work, on meeting deadlines and tackling problems. That was my drug. Without that, I had nothing. Just endless time to consider where I'd gone wrong.

The urge to call Sebastian was incredibly strong. I didn't even know if he'd answer, or what I'd say if he did. Nothing had changed between us. But I was desperate to hear that soothing voice, to wrap my arms around him and hold on for dear life before the weight of it all pulled me under.

But I restrained myself. I couldn't deal with any more heartbreak at the moment. Instead I popped a couple of Valium I had left over from my last international trip, and curled up on the couch.

For now, oblivion would do.

* * * * *

The letter arrived two days later.

For a while I just stared, unsure whether I should even open it. Seeing Sebastian's flowing script used to fill me with excitement, but now there was only trepidation. I wasn't sure I was ready to deal with whatever he had to say, not on top of everything else. This wasn't a reconciliation. You didn't fix our sorts of problems by post.

But in the end I knew I couldn't ignore it. Too much had passed between us for that. With trembling hands, I tore open the seal.

Sophia.

I'm sorry to do this in writing. I wanted to come to you — I nearly did several times — but I'm afraid of what will happen if I do. I always thought I was a strong man, but you have this way of making me feel utterly powerless. I'm worried I'll break yet again.

I'm so sorry that things have to end this way. It sounds hollow and empty, but I never meant to hurt you. I really thought that maybe I could do this again, that things would be different this time. But now I see how impossible that is. I can never have a normal life. The risks are just too great.

You have questions, but the answers I owe you aren't mine to give. It's not fair, but I need you to know that it's for the best. There is more at stake here than you can possibly imagine.

I know you probably don't believe me, but I want to tell you again: I never lied about my feelings for you. Every word was true. I never thought I'd care about anyone again the way I care about you. I thought Liv had burned that right out of me. But I was wrong. You're the most amazing woman I've ever met. I feel more in a day with you than I have in a lifetime with anyone

145

else. You deserve someone to share everything with, but that's not something I can give you, no matter how badly I want to. Perhaps it would have been better for both of us if I'd just stayed away to begin with. I knew you were dangerous from the moment I laid eyes on you. But I can't apologise. I don't regret a single moment we spent together.

I won't be in contact again. I ask that you please do the same. Like I said, it's for the best.

Yours forever.
-S

The room around me blurred into nothingness. All I could see were his words, blinking up at me like a neon sign. My organs felt like they'd been twisted into a thousand ragged knots inside me.

I no longer doubted that he'd been telling the truth about his feelings. I felt his passion right through to my bones. But that didn't matter anymore. Whatever his secrets were, they were apparently bigger than us, and they left no room in his life for anything more.

Despite the fact that I'd been expecting it, the finality of that last line ripped through me. Even after his office, with the weight of a thousand lies bearing down on us, some tiny part of me had still held hope that we'd get through it. There was a chance, however slim. But now that chance was over.

We were over.

Chapter 15

Time passed. I slept and ate and did my best to occupy myself, but it was all done with the kind of blank obligation that leaves next to no real impression. I felt so utterly disconnected, like I was watching a video of something that was happening to someone else.

I hated myself for being so weak. I'd never been one to wallow in self-pity before. Problems weren't things to dwell on, they were obstacles to be overcome on the way to better things. But in this situation, I didn't even know where to start.

I must have read Sebastian's note a hundred times over the next few days. It consumed me. I had no idea how one single piece of paper could make my heart soar so high yet still shatter into a million pieces. I wanted to hate him for not choosing me, but the way the letter was phrased made me question if he even had a choice at all. That scared me a little. The things he alluded to were every bit as unbelievable as those my imagination had conjured. Perhaps he really had been doing me a favour.

Eventually, after several days of ignoring my phone, I woke up one afternoon to find Ruth banging on my door.

"Holy shit," she said, when I finally answered. "You look like you've just returned from a week long bender."

"That good, huh?" I replied, managing a small smile. I'd thought I couldn't stomach company, but now that she was there in front of me, I realised how much I appreciated seeing a familiar face.

She stared at me, her brow furrowed in concern.

"So, word got around then I take it?" I asked.

She nodded. "Elle called me saying you weren't answering your phone. Explained what had happened. I came as soon as I could." She stepped towards me and pulled me into a hug. "I'm sorry, Soph."

I didn't know what to say, so I just hugged her back.

"Can I come in?" she asked. I nodded and lead her into the lounge.

"Now, tell me about it," she said.

And so I did, being careful to avoid mentioning Sebastian. She obviously had no idea about that, and it was still too raw for me to talk about.

When I was done, she let out a long breath and shook her head slowly. "I'll never understand how the people in that place are so blind. It's like it's all just a popularity contest. And if I ever meet that bitch Jennifer, she's going to need more than some weaselly little partner to hide behind."

I found myself grinning. Now *that* was what best friends were for. Making you feel like you weren't totally alone.

"So, there's no chance this will all just blow over?" she asked.

I shook my head slowly. "This is 'firing people 101'. Get them out of the building quietly, and then finish the job. And even if it wasn't, you can't work in a place like that when someone so senior has it out for you. Not unless you want to eat shit for the rest of your natural life."

Ruth nodded slowly, her mouth pulled tight. "Okay, so then we start out trying to find you something new. It sounds like Ernest wasn't on board with all this, right? So he'll write you an awesome reference. That plus a resume like yours and I bet you can stroll into any of the other big law firms in town." She looked thoughtful for a moment. "Maybe your mystery man could help out as well? If he knows one of the equity partners at Little Bell, he probably has other connections too."

I gazed at her, desperately willing my face to stay composed, but I couldn't hold it all back.

"Oh shit, not him too?" she asked.

I nodded.

She reached out and squeezed my shoulder. "Damn, the universe really knows how to kick a girl when she's down. I'm sorry, hon'. So he turned out to be an asshole after all?"

I blinked a few times. "I don't know. I don't think so. I'm still not really sure what happened." I sniffed sharply, realising that a few hot tears had begun to trace their way down my face. "Could we not talk about him? It won't make any difference. It's over. Maybe in a few months I'll be ready to laugh and dissect it with you and Lou over mojitos or something, but for now I think I just need to deal with it in my own way, okay?"

She hesitated. "Okay, sure. But just remember; I'm here if you change your mind."

"I know. Thanks."

She studied me for a few more seconds before clapping her hands. "You have, however, given me an idea. If there was ever a better excuse for midday mojitos, I haven't heard it."

I groaned. "I don't think going out and getting tanked at three o'clock on a Wednesday is the best way to start rebuilding my life."

"Who said anything about getting tanked? I'm just trying to get you out of the house. Have you even been outside since

149

it happened?"

I sighed, then shook my head.

"Exactly. So come out for one drink and some food that doesn't come out of a plastic packet. You'll never make any progress if you just hide out in here forever."

"I don't know, Ruth, I—"

"I'm not taking no for an answer," she interrupted. I knew there was no point in arguing. She was as stubborn as me when she wanted to be.

"Fine. One drink."

"Attagirl."

After taking a few minutes to shower and change into something half respectable, we headed for King Street. It felt surprisingly good to be out of the house. We found a little Tapas joint and settled in for lunch.

The longer we talked, the better I found myself feeling. It was inane conversation, mostly about Lou turning into a frumpy housewife, but that's exactly what the doctor ordered. I even laughed a few times, which I hadn't thought I'd be capable of anymore. It wasn't much more than a distraction, but it was a start.

* * * * *

Determined to begin regaining some semblance of control over my life, I made myself get up at nine the next morning. It was a tiny gesture, but at that moment every deliberate action felt like an achievement. Some bacon and eggs, a shower, and a lengthy grooming session later, I actually felt vaguely human.

I'd promised Ruth I wouldn't stay cooped up all day, so with nothing else on my schedule for the morning, I decided to take a walk. It was a lovely spring day outside, and I figured the sun might do me some good.

I wandered around Newtown for an hour or so, nabbing a coffee and a Danish in the process. It was nice just being outside among the hustle and bustle. It served as a reminder that despite how awful I felt, the world hadn't stopped turning. Things changed, and new opportunities were out there. I just had to find them.

Eventually, I headed home. The sooner I began hunting, the sooner I'd be able to start rebuilding my life. Snagging my mail from the letterbox, I strolled in through the front door, dumped it down on the sideboard, and headed for my laptop. It wasn't until I fired it up and sat down that I noticed anything was amiss. There was a breeze blowing into the room from the back door. The back door that now lay in a splintered mess on the kitchen floor.

It was one of those slow realisations that happens a fraction too late. An unexpected sight, a dumbfounded stare, and in the blink of an eye it's over. I sensed movement to my left, but before I could spin, something dark was slipped over my head and I felt a sharp jab on one side of my neck. I tried to yell for help, but whatever drug they'd injected me with worked fast. All I managed was a strangled squeal that cut off sharply as everything began to fade out.

About the Author

Maya Cross is a writer who enjoys making people blush. Growing up with a mother who worked in a book store, she read a lot from a very young age, and soon enough picked up a pen of her own. She's tried her hands at a whole variety of genres including horror, science fiction, and fantasy, but funnily enough, it was the sexy stuff that stuck. She has now started this pen name as an outlet for her spicier thoughts (they were starting to overflow). She likes her heroes strong but mysterious, her encounters sizzling, and her characters true to life.

She believes in writing familiar narratives told with a twist, so most of her stories will feel comfortable, but hopefully a little unique. Whatever genre she's writing, finding a fascinating concept is the first and most important step.

The Alpha Group is her first attempt at erotic romance.

When she's not writing, she's playing tennis, trawling her home town of Sydney for new inspiration, and drinking too much coffee.

Website: http://www.mayacross.com
Facebook: http://facebook.com/mayacrossbooks
Twitter: https://twitter.com/Maya_cross

Made in the USA
Lexington, KY
19 August 2014